PROSE FICTION

PROSE FICTION

*UEA Postgraduate
Creative Writing Anthology
2018*

CONTENTS

Foreword

In an attempt to look more intellectual I dyed my hair brown the week before starting my MA in Creative Writing at UEA. As a mature-ish student with a nursing background and no degree, let alone A Levels, to my name, I felt that radical change was necessary if I had any hope of fitting in. The MA sort – I suspected – would be wearing berets, smoking gold-tipped cigarettes and discussing Dostoevsky, and I wore almost exclusively end-of-season Topshop and read Jackie Collins.

I signed up full time but actually lived in London, had a two-year-old daughter, and a part-time community nursing job that I couldn't afford to leave, despite the generosity of the Malcolm Bradbury Bursary. I shared car journeys with a fellow student who was also commuting between two cities. We counted roadkill on those journeys. Strangely, there was an extraordinary amount on the A-road to Norwich, perhaps the reason for all the dead animals in our early work. Badgers and deer and foxes, we wrote about. Once, a talking duck.

The animals were bizarre and the people were too. We were misfits, all of us, but we worked as a group; it was like we were reliving *The Breakfast Club*. There were no berets after all, but Tadzio Koelb put the hip in hipster. My tutors were an eclectic bunch too, as unusual and bright and sometimes insecure as we all were. (I didn't realise the secret of publishing back then – that there really is no them and us.) But I was in awe, of course. I closed my eyes once during Trezza Azzopardi's workshop: her words were music.

My fellow students have gone on to do many different things, some you'll know about already: Naomi Wood and Anjali Joseph to name two. Others continue to write and are yet to be published. Regardless of when that happens, we are all writers who became friends and then, supporting each other through all the joys and tragedies of life which the subsequent ten years have brought, we became family. UEA does that to you.

I was back at UEA last week receiving an honorary Doctor of Letters. I smiled all the way there. I felt like I was going home. Norwich has changed a lot in ten years. It's become something of a Mecca for alternatives. Us misfits would have fitted right in. But on the road I counted roadkill: two rabbits, a pheasant and half a squirrel. Some things never change.

I have no doubt that this latest anthology contains the next big literary thing. But it will also hold the bizarre, the experimental, the simply fun examples of writing that is not yet influenced by Nielsen Book Scan numbers or marketing budgets. And in the white space between the pages are those UEA friendships strong enough to grow despite and because of all that's to come. There is freedom here, in these pages.

PHILIP LANGESKOV & NAOMI WOOD
Introduction

This is our first year as convenors of the MA in Prose Fiction, inheriting the mantle from Jean McNeil and Henry Sutton who, for five years, ensured that this fine course continued to prosper. We feel the honour keenly, not least because we are both graduates of the programme. We know a little, then, about what it can mean for writers to make their way – this year, from the Philippines, the United States, Australia, Canada, Trinidad and Germany, India and the Republic of Ireland, as well as the UK and Northern Ireland – to this glorious concrete campus on the leafy fringes of Norwich. We know the trepidation that attends arrival; perhaps most of all, we know the thrill that such an experience brings with it: a whole year, to read, to think, *to write*. If you're the kind of person for whom such things matter, it's a rare gift.

The writers who come here enter into a lineage. It is a lineage made up of the writers, teachers, thinkers and critics who have passed through this place. Many of them are famous, many more of them are not, but they have all played a part in establishing the atmosphere of intense commitment and collaborative creative endeavour that makes this course such a pleasure to be associated with. One of those writers, Sir Kazuo Ishiguro, reflected in his 2017 Nobel Prize acceptance speech that what he found when he came to Norwich in the autumn of 1979 was 'an unusual amount of quiet and solitude in which to transform myself into a writer.' Much has changed since then. Norwich is possibly less quiet; the course has altered, too, grown in size and, perhaps, in stature. It remains the case, however, that this is a time – and a place – of transformation.

As this year has rolled on, we have watched, with considerable delight, as every one of the writers in this anthology has found a way to flourish, to grow, each of them grappling in the dark for a surer way of articulating their own experience of being in the world. For some, their work has radically changed. Provoked into a grand reassessment, some have decided to scrap one novel and start another, to swap genre or form. Short story writers have turned into novelists, novelists have turned into short story writers. A few, in hours of need, have turned to poetry. Others have perhaps changed more incrementally: sharpening their sentences, building the architecture of their plots, settling on a style. All of this, in whatever quantities and combinations, is encouraged. A willingness to takes risks is a welcome attribute.

And the risk required is not always a question of imaginative daring. If you were to look back over the introductions that have prefaced these annual anthologies, you will find one word that crops up again and again: privilege – the privilege of being here; the privilege of teaching; the privilege of a year free, as much as possible, from the encumbrances of everyday living. That privilege doesn't come cheap; it is not, regrettably, available to everyone. For many of the writers who come here, to do so requires sacrifices of various kinds – financial, familial, social; then there are the other writers, the ones for whom sacrifice was not an option, who didn't make it here at all. To mitigate the risks, we have several sources of funding available; the dream, actively pursued, is one day to be able to offer funding of one kind or another to every writer who longs to come here. With that aim in mind, this year we have been able to introduce two new scholarships to our already significant donor-funded scholarship programme – one through the generosity of the Miles Morland Foundation, to support a writer from Africa; another, through the excellent crowdfunding efforts of Louise Doughty, to support a BAME writer from the UK. These are vital interventions. A lineage that looks only backwards, or inwards, towards itself, will not change anything, no matter how storied it may be. We need new names, new voices, to break us open again, and to jolt us out of those styles, those ways of being, we have become accustomed to calling familiar. We are grateful beyond measure to the many funders whose generosity enables us to give those new names and voices a space in which to think and breathe and dream.

Those voices lie, waiting, in the future, pleasures to be discovered. For now, in the present, we come back to the writers of 2017-18, on both our MA and MFA programmes. They know who they are and you soon will too. As much as anything, this is a year of experiment and play. As we discover, time and again, the writers who come here are agile and hungry; ready to react and change when thrown fresh challenges, or when the world shows them something new and compels them to catch it. Inside this anthology you will find the evidence of that agility in a startling portfolio of voices that shows this cohort's extraordinary ambition and brilliance. These are pieces of fiction in many hues, some elegantly turned and patient, some racingly propulsive, others raw; in them all, the past rubs up against the present to create the future, in its many imaginary possibilities. This talented bunch have given us an easy year of managing the course for the first time. We are grateful to them – for their words, yes, but also for their fierce commitment and energy, their good humour, and their willingness to take the risk of coming here in the first place. As we say – and mean – each year: this place doesn't make writers; the writers make this place.

Finally, with the weather as it is at the time of writing – a hot and windy July – we are reminded of a wonderful formulation of writing given by another Nobel Laureate, Orhan Pamuk, in which he describes the pleasures of being a writer on the way to writing something good as being like the sailor who, when becalmed, feels the first twitch of wind on his arm: the sails are about to fill, the boat is about to move, out of the harbour, to the sea and on towards the horizon.

This diverse anthology comprises the latest work from the 2018 cohort of prose fiction writers studying UEA's renowned Creative Writing MA and MFA.

Harriet Avery works at a library in Suffolk. Her writing has been published in *The Red Line, Henshaw Press* and *Electric Reads*, amongst other places. This extract is the opening of her current novel-in-progress. It takes as inspiration the life of Rosalind Franklin – the scientist who was overlooked for her crucial work on DNA's helical structure – and spans different decades, continents and voices. The focus falls on Franklin after she left the world of DNA, but also imagines the lives of two other women, her mother and her nurse, ultimately forming a meditation on motherhood, choice and the nature of being a woman, set in a time when what it meant to be a woman was changing.

Double Helix
Extract from a novel

1956 – R

It was only when we arrived in Joshua Lederberg's motorcar, and they were all running down the path to greet us, that it really struck me – the enormity of it. The enormity of the situation.

How did I not see it before? How can I have been so stupid? It's as if I have been living in a daze, all this time – too caught up with the conference circuit, and meeting friends, and making sure I spoke to all the necessary people.

I didn't notice that *you* had wormed your way into my mind – into existence, taking on a life of your own, for yourself – I thought that you were just a fleeting notion, weeks ago – the sort of thought that I suppose most girls have, now and then – and now I turn around and find we have leapt from passing thought to something which is apparently entirely solid and anchored and fixed inside me. (Yes, tentacles like those jellyfish we saw washed up on Half Moon Bay, blue string, pushing all through me, through all my tracts and bones, into every possible nook and cranny, twisted around, unable, now, to be extricated at *all*.)

Bypassed all the moments when I might have quenched you, quite happily, with rationality and common sense. Telling myself not to be ridiculous. Now I'm stuck with you, and I don't know what to do.

I don't know what to do.

But wait. Let's just slow down. Think about this logically.

Of course it cannot really be the case. You don't exist. If you are just a thought, I can get rid of you, as easily as that.

Because I simply *thought* of you, back in California. California in late July: the sun was hot enough to melt the tarmac, and the tyres on the cars, these huge American cars, which take half an hour simply to walk around. Everything here is large – a cliché – but it is one of those clichés which is rooted in fact. The roads in Berkeley are simply too wide to be believed. Such an air of space, as if the sun itself is forcing everything to hold itself apart – in the same way as one holds one's arms a little apart from one's sides when it is too hot for words. So different to cramped London. I thought it the first time I came, and it proves not to have changed. Not that I expected it to. Perhaps I am the one who has changed.

It was my birthday while I was there. The twenty-fifth of July. Now I am thirty-six. Thirty-six years old. Hard to believe. (I wonder if other people have the same unreal feeling: a feeling that one is not actually more than a girl, that at least twenty of those thirty-six years were not real, but a slip in time, somehow. I catch myself, now and again – like meeting the glance of one's own reflection unexpectedly in a glass out of the corner of one's eye – looking around for someone else to make a decision, or at least affirm that the decision taken is the right one. And then back at Birkbeck, Kenneth and John stand and look at me expectantly, and I realise, no, the judgement must be mine. That's how it is. In reality, I am used to it. The girl has to be hidden away, if she cannot be discarded entirely.)

Thirty-six. Old, I suppose, to be facing this. Facing you, as you are.

Stop that! It's not the case. Simply cannot be, that's all.

I had such a lovely birthday in Berkeley. We went out to Stouffer's, where we had the vegetable plate, filet mignon steak with a wonderful peppercorn dressing (soaked up every last drop with the bread and butter) and then a baked raspberry cheesecake. (I can still taste it, soft and creamy and delicious. I've never had baked cheesecake before.) It wasn't specifically for my birthday – we were going to eat out, anyhow – but the Tessmans found out, and they got everyone to chip in and pay for mine, and a bottle of Cabernet Sauvignon for me as well. Of course any one of them could have paid for it on their own – the point was to share it, as a gift from them, to me. It's nice to feel one has friends.

Americans are awfully generous as a rule, even with research – outside of Berkeley, anyway, where they are rather overly competitive – not the only lab in the world to be so, in my experience.

We walked home from Stouffer's, which is rare enough for these Americans – but I suppose they were a little merry with the wine, and the good food – I often feel that good food can make one almost as squiffy as alcohol – so we walked – a warm blue night, and the sky above very clear – the stars were just like a spray of luminescence, all in different places than I expected. A different planet. It quite reminded me of the sky from the top of a mountain – the sense that I could step up into it, and simultaneously that it is so very far away – but I've never seen it like that from a city street before.

We came across students from the university dancing on the pavement outside a bar called The Duke. Ethel dragged Irwin to join in as we went by – the rest laughed at them – but I noticed how the moon, which was very strong, glinted from the tops of Irwin's shoes, and in Ethel's hair, making silver shines. There is something of science about moonlight – like the lights in a lab. I suppose most people would find that a rather cold thing to think. But I mean that it is clarifying.

They asked me to dance with them – teased me, really. All in jest. But I couldn't. Of course I couldn't.

Was it that night that it happened, or was it the following evening? – I forget now. It's hardly important. Certainly, three weeks ago, or thereabouts, when I was staying with the Levensons. It may well have been that precise evening, after we walked from Stouffer's. The episode itself is vivid in my memory. I was just leaving the kitchen, where I had gone to fetch a glass of water.

But I think – yes – there were moments – even earlier than that – moments where I did feel strange. That time when we went to see the sequoias in the Calaveras Park – just myself and Ethel and Irwin, and Renato Dulbecco – Renato is in the front room at this instant. I can hear him below, talking with Joshua Lederberg. Anyway, he was there with us.

In the Park, we ate our picnic, all four of us in a single nook of a single tree-trunk – that's how large they were, those old, wise, majestic trees, like kings, somehow, real old mythic kings – or gods. We all, without agreeing or thinking about it, spoke more softly than usual. One only gently touches that ancient bark, with something like reverence.

But we did eat late – I ate rather quickly. Which explains the nausea. Doesn't it? I thought so, at the time. Bubbles in the stomach is just indigestion. (That's what I said to the doctor.) But now – now I wonder if – already, it was you.

You made it difficult for me to properly admire the stillness of the light, and the veins and the sinews of the trees – strange to think of them as living beings, even though there was a sense of enormous *life* there – and to think they might be connected, however distantly, to the little leaves and stems of the tobacco plants, with which we are all so familiar in our labs. One could not possibly dissect one of those trees. Crystallise the individual cells. Aside from the impracticality, there is something in me which resists the idea completely. Do I mean that those trees are beyond science? No. But they are something separate, something enclosed – I can hardly describe it. Some of those giants were apparently more than two thousand years old. Imagine all they have seen, and experienced. No wonder they felt so wise.

What a stupid human thing, I thought, to be in that natural beautiful wonderful place, and to have spoiled it all by eating too fast.

Except that if it wasn't indigestion, after all – and perhaps neither was that other time, with Robley in Gunther Stent's lab – but that was after lunch, again, and a very rich lunch. It could have simply disagreed with me. It was just a feeling of sickness, that's all. Why should I have thought anything more about it? Nothing occurred to me, at the time. Not in so many words.

On my birthday night, back at the Levensons' house – what a house, the Levensons' house! – set at the top of that hill looking down over the bay – I would have been convinced that it was an hotel, except that the neighbouring properties, all along the Stonewall Road, are equally marvellous – the Levensons' a smooth, white, quite modern affair, very tall and stately, large enough to have wings, although the rooms inside are so vast and spacious in themselves, that it has only really a normal amount of rooms for a moderate family. Rosemary says that she wants to have another two children, preferably another boy for Richard and another girl for Irene. It seems a strange thing. In my head, I have an abiding impression of Rosemary – we hardly know each other, but she is my distant cousin, one of the Sebag-Montefiores – as the little fat blonde girl who curtsied to her own father, the colonel, outside Grandpa's synagogue, with the toe of her white shoe scraping a large circle across the pavement, and her hands pulling out the sides of her blue sailor skirt – she must have been six, I, fourteen.

But why should it be strange for her, now? After all, David is a father now. And Colin and Roland want children, certainly. Of course, it's much easier for the men. It doesn't have to be a choice for them.

Anyway, the point is that I was alone in the Levensons' kitchen. They were all in bed. And the house is quite ridiculously large, so I was completely isolated. If I had called for help, I daresay I would not have been heard.

And what would they have done, if they all came running? Frankly embarrassing if they had. It was alarming at the time, but really hardly worth making a fuss.

I shall recount it exactly as it was. Because now I want to see it completely. The hypothesis is there. *You*. So let's see if the evidence stacks up from the start.

I came in, after dinner, my birthday – quite late, perhaps eleven or twelve o'clock. Rosemary had given me a key, so I let myself in. The house was darkened, and silent. The maid leaves all the downstairs doors open, so there were all sorts of interesting shadows from the moon coming through the doorways and between the bannisters, strange shapes on the walls. Shadows always interest me so.

I noticed immediately the little chips of refracted light overlaying the wallpaper in a fine scatter pattern, like a handful of marbles thrown – the source could be traced easily back to the chandelier hanging over the staircase, where the moonlight refracted through the hanging glass diamonds. Looking very closely, the little ha'pennies of light were tinted just slightly here and there – by the bureau at the bottom step, there was one which was clearly but faintly red, as if someone had just dabbed the spot, just once, with rouge, as Mother wears. Coral rouge. The division of the light spectrum.

I was happy. It was my birthday. I was having a fine time. Was there some feeling of discomfort? I believe there was, but I had just eaten steak and cheesecake – so of course, I was full. Contentedly full.

I took off my coat and shoes – I went through the hall in my stockings to the back of the house, where the kitchen is. I was thirsty. Yes, a very dry mouth, I remember. The dinner was heavily salted, I suppose, and the alcohol, of course... I took a glass from the cupboard, filled it from the tap. Looked out of the window – I could hardly see a thing of the garden, which was quite wild with trees and the steepness of the hill – I saw my reflection. I think I was startled by it, not because I looked especially pale, but more the fact that there was this face, looking suddenly straight back at me.

GEMMA BARRY

Gemma Barry is the 2017/18 recipient of the David Higham Award and was a finalist for Glimmer Train's September/October 2017 Short Story Award for New Writers. She has a degree in American and English Literature, also from UEA.

Out to Sea, More Things are Swimming
Extract from a novella

I've started roaming on the beach at night. I like the lonely, lunar way it makes me feel, and how the night turns a blind eye. By day, I feel overexposed. I feel as though the sun is lighting up my bones, and I have to think very carefully about walking, the sheer mechanics of it. At night, I don't have an X-ray vision of myself. I take great strides across the bay. I jump off sandbanks. I run at the dark like a waterproof ghoul. In the eyes of society, these aren't legitimate hobbies, but nor is napping in the bath, or Googling your primary school nemesis to discover that she is now a PE teacher.

Once, walking home, I saw torchlight in the distance, a thin beam along the sand that made me stop and crouch down. I had to press my palms on the sand to steady myself, and then I was gripping great handfuls of it, watching the beam get closer and closer until I could hear the swish-swish of synthetic trousers. Prickled with sweat, I got a giddy feeling, like playing Murder In The Dark in somebody's cramped living room when you can hear the stifled breath of the Murderer and you yourself try to stop breathing. If the beam had found me, what then? How could we have explained ourselves? Only certain types of people go to the beach at night. I think, like me, they are trying to disappear.

There are beaches for roaming and beaches for reclining. I live at the edge of a roaming beach on the south coast of the island, where the air has a sewery tinge and the sand is coarse and shaly, studded with broken shells that look like toenail clippings. It is not like the fine, white powder you get on the west coast. There the bikini girls unfurl on tropical-coloured towels and the sand sticks to their hinds like sugar on doughnuts. They smell, collectively, like fake coconuts and virgin daiquiris and the security that comes from never having sweated into the arms of anything. Such blithe creatures! My beach attracts shambling, rain-coated men with metal detectors, lone dog-walkers, and – when the light shrinks westward – teenagers swigging from bottles, weaving through the rocks on their way to town. I don't know what we smell like. Wet fur and cheap wine, maybe.

I live alone, the most womanish thing about me. My house is situated at the very end of the promenade, and shares none of its Victorian grandeur.

It's small and clapboard and has the just-habitable air of a beach hut. I imagine that, if you licked the house, it would taste like salt. I have never licked the house, though the idea crosses my mind when the morning sun shines on the peeling paint, and there is a certain smell in the air. Once, on a family holiday to France, I licked the inside part of a cathedral. I had pressed my right eye against a keyhole (the forbidden, cordoned-off parts of public buildings are always the most intriguing) and, with my face so close to the smooth wedge of wooden door, I had stuck out my tongue. I can't explain why. I suppose I wanted to see if the door tasted as damp and historical as it smelt. For the rest of the day I had a bitter taste in my mouth, as though a copper penny was fizzing under my tongue.

If the rumours are true, the house used to be a brothel, though I can't find evidence to support this theory, not in books or microfiche copies of the local newspaper. More recently it was a guesthouse. I've repainted the sign above the door, the one that says NO VACANCIES, and there it swings, on two short chains – not proudly, exactly, but certainly with a renewed sense of vigour. At night, when the breeze picks up off the black sea, I hear it creaking back and forth below my bedroom window, and it fills me with an indefinable sense of dread. By day, I think the sign is quite witty, especially when my brothers visit, bringing with them their wives and their children and their noise. I make the same joke each time, pointing at the sign and saying, 'Can't you read?' and pretending that they can't come inside. We laugh every time at that old routine.

I have a notion that I might restore the guesthouse to its former glory, open it for business once again, and become the type of person who can operate in enterprising and successful ways. I picture myself the smiling feature of a newspaper article: LOCAL WOMAN TRANSFORMS HISTORIC BEACH HOUSE. This same woman goes about making beds and breakfasts for strangers, all the while being convivial and obliging, in flagrant contravention of her true self. Her true self is slovenly. Her true self objects to making breakfasts. Breakfast is an antidepressant pressed into a hard-boiled egg, and it's usually eaten at lunchtime.

—

Neil comes in on the morning boat. Since I moved here, he makes a habit of regular visits – perhaps they are too regular and he is checking up on me out of fraternal concern. I meet him at the harbour, standing awkwardly among the day trippers waiting to board the vacated boat, which will part great waves back towards the mainland, reeking of vomit and cider and stale air. There are always drunks on the morning boat. They come here looking for a good time, but their revelry begins out to sea, before most people have even contemplated coffee. They get lairy and loud, sloshing about from side to side. I detest the sight of them, because I have been that brash person before, laughing and drinking and not caring about some solitary woman standing by, narrowing her eyes.

I see Neil first, then Josh. It is always easier when he brings Josh. Two adults will naturally orbit a child, even a quiet one who doesn't demand much in the way of attention and operates on a cool plain of quiet decorum.

'How are you?' I ask, hugging them in turns.

Josh has reluctantly ceased playing a handheld game. He holds it at his side, trying to deny its existence. He looks like a miniature version of Neil, which is to say he looks like a short-haired version of me when I was a little girl. We all have the same colour hair, which is a pale brown, almost grey, but theirs curls and turns golden after five minutes in the sun.

'Fine,' says Neil. He is a man of few words. When you get him drunk, he offers up a few more. He has a solemn, self-conscious intellect that I occasionally find frustrating. 'You look tired,' he says, to which I can only shrug.

I suggest going to the aquarium, which is at the end of the pier and whose entrance is built to look like a giant fish head, with two blank eyes and a gaping, red-lipped mouth. You step through the mouth into a series of caverns – the fish cavern, the mollusc cavern. The walls are rough as real coral and sunk with hidden speakers piping vague, instrumental songs that do nothing to evoke the sea, but instead make you think of panpipes being played on a keyboard in a studio by someone who saw their life going in a different direction.

'Have you been here before?' I ask Josh. 'Has your daddy brought you here before?'

'My dad hasn't,' he says.

He lets me hold his hand, which is small and sticky. I want to crush it. It is the same feeling I get when I scoop up Pilgrim and she puts her little paws against my collarbone, and I know that I could squeeze the life out of her.

I've noticed that, at the aquarium, people move slowly, as if they, too, are underwater. I think we are all struck dumb by the sight of that cold mass pressing against the reinforced glass. The children streak their hands on the glass, making mucky little comet tails, and sometimes they pound on it, and the chambers fill briefly with the sound of their tiny fists banging. I sometimes wonder how many people are looking at the fish, and how many people are looking at the further reaches of the tank – the dark recesses, the coral alcoves – and seeing the beauty of having so much to hide behind.

Josh strains to peer into a tank of seahorses. I pick him up and we watch them together. There are seven or eight of them, all a sort of caustic yellow. They swim clumsily, floating and bumping about like astronauts defying gravity for the first time. Some have anchored themselves by wrapping their tails around fronds and coral and clinging for dear life. They are all caught in the eternal, never-ending storm of the filter, which sits in the top corner of the tank and bubbles the water ceaselessly, creating mini riptides. What a chaos they have to endure! I peer into their beady, beseeching eyes. Yes, yes, we are all just clinging on.

'Do you know,' Josh says, 'that daddy seahorses have babies?'

'Are you sure?' I say. I think it sounds unlikely.

'They cough them out,' he says. 'Or they come out of the daddy's nose and it helps him swim.'

I don't know what to say. The seahorses remind me of a time many years ago, walking on the beach with a man whose present life I know nothing about. The sand was wet and rugged where the tide had pulled back over it, and we were following the sea out, over many miles, collecting cockles in a bucket. We spotted a tiny pipefish, undulating in a crater of saltwater no bigger than a footprint. Neither he nor I had seen one before, and we reacted simultaneously with surprise and delight. That is the thing I recall most vividly – not the marvel of the pipefish, but the marvel of our noticing it at the same time, as if our eyes looked out on the same world, and our bodies were perfectly synchronised and finely attuned to all the small wonders it had to offer.

'I'm going to find my dad now,' Josh says, wriggling free.

We find Neil in the gift shop, fingering a large, serrated tooth from a basket of identical ones. A label says SHARK TEETH but they look too glossy to be real. Plus whose job would it be to harvest them?

'This is actually pretty cool,' he says, pushing his finger against the point. He pretends to gash the face of his son. They both laugh. Josh's attention turns elsewhere, but Neil seems reluctant to part with the tooth.

'Don't you have enough pocket money?' I say.

Outside, we get fish and chips for lunch. We eat them standing on the pier, salty and wind-whipped, while the waves froth violently beneath us.

'How are things?' Neil asks.

'Fine,' I say. 'Good.'

'You're not lonely in the house?'

'No,' I say. 'Plus I have a cat.'

Some nights I do not sleep alone, but with a man named Jam – short for James – whom I have known since I was seventeen. He comes over at night, smelling of cigarettes and booze, and we lie in the dark with the windows pushed open, letting the salt air in. We talk about small, often silly things. I do not love him, or his company, or even the sexual aspect of his presence. He reminds me of a simpler time, and that is all.

'Are you enjoying your fish and chips?' I say to Josh.

He nods. 'Hey,' he says, brightly. 'We looked at fish, and now we're eating fish.'

'That's right,' I say, swallowing.

'Fish swimming in our bellies,' he says.

He does not seem at all perturbed.

S. C. Bayat was born in Manchester and moved to Vancouver Island, Canada, at the age of nine. In 2016, she was longlisted for the Prism International Short Fiction Contest and was a semi-finalist for the Raymond Carver Short Story Contest. She was the recipient of the University of East Anglia's North American Bursary in 2017. Her stories have appeared in *Little Fiction*, *The Dalhousie Review*, *Prism International*, and *The Malahat Review*. She is currently working on her first novel, an extract of which appears here.

Bruisers
Extract from a novel

When you hit a man, you have to hold your heart in your fist or he won't feel it. The heart is key in this exchange. You've to mean what you say, and say it with enough force that he'll listen. And don't give him the chance to answer back. Keep your hands up and your feet moving, and you'll keep him mute. This is what Antony Morran tells the brash boys of Barnsley, Yorkshire, right before they're knocked, one-by-inevitable-one, on their newly humbled arses.

In the bleak schoolyard of Abbott Hill Secondary, bodies swarm round a spectacle. They clamour over and under and around one another to get a look at what they've come for. Frankie Bonham, current champion, is defending his title against Seamus Hoult, resident Pooh-Bah and renowned dickhead. At sixteen, weighing in at 160lbs and at a towering 5'9" tall, Hoult is a crowd favourite compared to Frankie, fourteen, who stands at a measly 5'4", 125lbs. They exchange a few quick palms to the shoulders and chest, and then Hoult goes for Frankie's neck, wraps a thick arm around it and swings him down. Within moments, Hoult has Frankie underneath him. The mob heckles louder. Hoult pins Frankie's arms, then his legs. The weight of Hoult carries through his fingers, and Frankie lies mashed between him and the ground.

'Blubberin' Bonham, that's what we'll call tha.' Hoult's mouth is a wide pit. His wisdom teeth are in; the lower left is black. His hair is tinged with orange, bulldog face pale and fleshy. 'Bonham the bastard.' There is a birthmark between his right eye and hairline that is shaped like a peanut and the colour of a skid mark. Saliva pools in his lower lip. 'Or Frankie the fairy, just like your dad.'

'Shut your face.' White heat swells beneath Frankie's skin and stiffens his limbs. His body is pinched into pimpled concrete, tenderising what little muscle is on him. He needs to get back on his feet if he's got any hope of winning.

Frankie tries to buck, but Hoult bears down harder. His thick head looks to the crowd, and he lets out a gull-ish laugh.

'He probably cries himself to sleep at night.' There are puny wires of hair beneath Hoult's chin; three, five at most. Still more than Frankie's got.

Frankie thrashes his head, feels the back of his scalp scrape like a match against the ground.

'Weetle Fwankie, sobbing for Daddy.'

He wants to claw that git-smirk right off Hoult. '*Fuck* you.'

Hoult's eyes narrow. 'That's no way for a little girl to talk.'

He shifts forward, swampy breath hitting the skin of Frankie's nose, his lip, fouling the air between their faces.

'Such an undignified way to die, in a pit. I bet he cried just like you do. I bet his weetle wip trembled—'

Too far, fuckhead.

Frankie spits. The phlegmy glob lands by Hoult's mouth. Hoult reacts, delight replaced by disgust, and herein lies his error: he wipes quickly at his jaw. Frankie's left arm is freed, and in an instant he uses it. Fist to bone, right on that peanut-shit mark. Hoult is knocked off balance. He throws an arm to steady himself against the concrete, and Frankie's right knuckles smash into Hoult's chin. In seconds, Frankie is out from under him and his knee is crunching the cartilage of Hoult's nose.

There is nothing in Headmaster Roberts's tidy office to distract Louise Bonham from the fact that she's been waiting for nearly fifteen minutes, having come in between shifts for an 'emergency meeting.' She is of the mind that people be bloody well on time for their appointments, particularly if it's to do with her son, and particularly if she isn't told what in particular about her Frankie warrants such urgency. She could be peeling russets and carrots for dinner, then take a much-needed doze before her five p.m. shift at The Sow's Ear, where she'll remain until after closing at eleven p.m. and then rise seven hours later to work a sewing machine at the Kangol hat factory. Instead, she's sat on a thinly cushioned chair on the other side of a very deep, almost bare desk, which stands in front of a bookshelf filled with what appear to be encyclopaedias. On the only wall shelf is a plate commemorating the birth of Prince William last year, which she'd seen advertised for a fortune in the paper at the end of summer. The man could at least hang a proper picture, for God's sake, introduce some colour to all this stale oak. Oh, enough, she thinks. Don't be a witch just because you're tired. She catches sight of herself reflected upside down in a vase on the desk, the porcelain glazed and filled with dusty stems of dried willow. Red-brown hair that resembles a large clump of hanging tree moss, which splays from beneath her wool hat and sits on her shoulders. A modest mouth cast down at the corners only somewhat, though it's enough to pull at the cheeks and eyes. Irises the colour of amber gemstones, but now without their loveliness. Where did it go? She stretches her mouth open wide and lets it fall into a smile, but she sees its hollowness and feels foolish, and it slips away.

The door opens, and Mr Roberts, tall and slim, strides hurriedly to his seat behind the desk. Louise sits up straighter and places her elbows on the armrests of her chair.

'*So* very sorry to keep you waiting, Mrs Bonham.' He unbuttons his suit jacket and straightens his tie, both brown. He's not Yorkshire born, but sounds much further south; London folk.

Louise raises an eyebrow.

'I was caught up in speaking with Mr Hoult about, well, about your son,' Mr Roberts says.

'Who's Mr Hoult?'

Mr Roberts flips open a cardstock file on his desk and begins to leaf through loose pieces of paper. He scratches carefully at his peppered moustache just beneath the nose, which is the width of a pencil at its bridge and a shot glass at its end. 'Frankie was involved in *another* fight this afternoon, and—'

'He's been in more than one?' She laughs when she says this – a quick, short gust – though she doesn't know why. 'I doubt it.' Her tone is dismissive, she knows, rude even, but this man has some gall.

'We've sent numerous letters.'

'My Frankie doesn't fight.'

'If you'd read the letters—'

'He doesn't.'

Mr Roberts folds his hands together in a manner that suggests authority. Louise crosses her own so that they're suspended between the chair's arms, held just above her lap.

'Mrs Bonham.' His tone is sharper now, the words more decided. 'You think your son is a good boy, but the fact remains this school has no tolerance for antagonistic behaviour.'

'Just what tha saying?'

'The letters give fair warning—'

'Bollocks, letters.'

'Expulsion, Mrs Bonham.'

Louise drops her elbows and back and jaw. When she speaks, she's quiet as night. 'Pardon?'

'Mr Hoult is a policeman. Frankie broke the nose of his son this afternoon.' Mr Roberts pauses – an arrogant pause – then continues. 'He very graciously understands the way teenage boys can be, and doesn't intend to pursue charges. But it's of his opinion, and mine, that Frankie is heading down a bad path, one that does not have a place within the walls of Abbott Hill.'

Louise feels her chin begin to tremble and covers it with her hand. 'How long has this gone on?' The pulse in her neck thumps hot.

Mr Roberts shifts in his chair. 'Obviously, there have been recent...' He clears his throat, a soft, useless noise. 'Events, in Frankie's life that have perhaps led to his acting out.'

Of course, Louise thinks, of course Frankie's not coping. After four months of stupor it's as if she's woken up. Of course not. What kind of mother would believe that he is? What kind of mother doesn't know? You, Louise reasons, you're the kind of mother. And then she begins to sob, hiccupped, deep cries, and she covers her face with both hands so that Mr Roberts cannot see her.

After some moments Mr Roberts stands and exits, returns with a box of tissues and places it gingerly on Louise's lap. He lingers, awkward, or maybe he thinks it comforting, and then takes a seat on the edge of his desk and crosses his legs, and waits. When she finally does calm, he offers her the wastebasket so that she can remove the pile of soiled tissues from her legs, then returns to his chair behind the desk.

'I have no desire to be the villain, Mrs Bonham.'

Louise pulls another tissue from the box and holds it taut between her hands. She widens her eyes to get a good look at it, tears stoppered in her eyelashes.

Mr Roberts shifts in his chair. 'Mrs Bonham.'

'Please don't make him leave.'

Mr Roberts sighs – contemplation, or perhaps exasperation, worn on his face. 'We'll make a deal.' He speaks to the ceiling above Louise's head. 'Get Frankie's behaviour under control and he may remain at Abbott Hill on a conditional basis.' He looks at her now, as he might one of his students. '*Any* more trouble and he's *absolutely* gone.'

Louise nods, wipes at her nose, and then stands. She leaves without another word.

For forty-two years, Red Knuckle Boxing Club has taught lads to be men. Antony Morran was raised here, among the stale leather and steely-jawed kids, and the pummelled spirits of callow bodies that bob and lurch with one another beneath dim overhanging bulbs. Paul Morran had quit mining coal and opened Knuckles soon after Antony, the youngest of five and his only son, were born. Four years later, Paul's wife left with the girls to start a new life in Manchester – *pissin' Manchester*? – with a conservative twat who diddled in civil service. She wasn't to take Antony though, not if she didn't want Paul making life difficult for her. A boy needs a man – a real man – to show him how to carry himself proper, and Paul was damned if he'd let any son of his be raised not knowing how to slug. He'd had gloves on Antony before the boy could read.

Paul had done right. By the time Antony was nineteen, he'd won enough amateur bouts to get noticed by the kinds of people who had their hands in decent fights. But a boxer can't go pro without a manager and a father can only train his son so far, and a pro needs a cut man, needs equipment, needs to spend, and all their money was tied up in the gym, so it had to go. Paul sold the lot of it to an Irish bloke who could no more box than tango, and it barbed more than he thought it would, handing over the keys. But his Antony would pull enough in the big time to get it back for him within the year, he knew. They'd pay double if they had to, they'd be that rich.

Aye, there's not many lads round here who escape the pits, or leave Yorkshire, for that matter. But young Antony'd done things his way. It had been an unexpected thing, then, his quiet return to Barnsley at the age of thirty, one that did not go unnoticed. When he bought back Knuckles eleven years (and almost as many owners) after he'd left, he found they'd let it ruin. Antony had taken care in the rebuilding, and had mostly done it alone, only calling in tradesmen to rewire the electrical that someone along the line had botched too spectacularly to fix himself. It had taken longer to finish than he'd expected, but he liked the quiet, the purposefulness of it all, and these are things that build back spirits as much as they do boxing gyms.

Rick Bland came to writing via a career as an actor – he was a long-time member of the Reduced Shakespeare Company and wrote, acted and produced his award-winning play *THICK*. His novel, *The Aftermath*, is a black comedy that charts the chaos within a working-class Canadian family before and after a fractious divorce.

The Aftermath
Non-sequential excerpts from a novel

1974

I remember when our cleaning lady, Mrs Riley, told Mum our house was a pigsty. Mum turned into a statue, her mouth a straight line, her eyes melty and cold. A few minutes later, Mum handed Mrs Riley her sandwich. Mrs Riley ate it like the cookie monster and turned red and started sweating, saying her sandwich was a bit too spicy for her liking.

Mum said, 'I'm sorry to hear that.'

And I saw Mum push the Tabasco behind the sugar. Mrs Riley didn't see it because she was too busy complaining in her Frosted-Lucky-Charms voice. Mum was like a giant next to Mrs Riley, who was as short and round as my friend Janet-the-Planet.

When Mrs Riley finally left, Mum exploded with words, none of them dirty but all of them hot and pointy. All that week Dad kept saying, 'We can always find another cleaning lady.'

'Jim, it took months to find Mrs Riley.'

'I'm just pointing out that you have options.'

'She needs to understand that she's expendable.'

'Is she?'

'Of course not, but she doesn't need to know that.'

'I bet the next time she comes, you'll kill her with kindness?'

Dad was right. The more Mum hated someone, the nicer she was to them, which made me happy because Mum was never *too* nice to us. That was how I knew she loved us so much.

The night before Mrs Riley returned, Mum cleaned our whole house. My brothers and me walked into the kitchen and saw Mum scrubbing the floor in her short shorts, her bum facing us. Tommy pointed to the hair popping out of Mum's underwear and I laughed when he whispered, *'Looks like bozo lady.'*

'What are you boys laughing about?' Mum said.

'Nothing,' Tommy said.

Mum only had a few hairs sticking out but whenever Mrs Black came to swim, Tommy would say it looked like bozo's wig was trying to escape from her bikini.

That was when Mum said, 'Get out of my hair,' and I learned that I could die from laughing.

Then Dad came into the kitchen and said, 'Marnie, leave Mrs Riley something to do tomorrow.'

'This floor needs to be spotless, so when Lady Riley complains, I'll serve her sandwich on it.'

'No, you won't.'

'Just wait, honestly Jim, just watch me.'

'Mummy, will you weally make Mrs Wiley eat off the floor?' Timmy said.

'Will you weally, Mummy. It's weally mean!' Tommy said.

'Don't. Tease. Your. Brother. How many times do I have to tell you?'

'Sixty-one.'

'Oh God, you're such a comedian,' Mum said.

We were watching *Hawaii Five-0* when Mum said *bed time,* in a sing-song voice. Mum walked to the couch and picked up Timmy. 'Did you hear me?'

'Can't we watch the whole show just once?'

'No, Trevor. Bed.'

'You're so unfair,' Tommy said.

'Bed. Now.'

Mum carried Timmy to his room so we kept watching TV, but because Timmy was already asleep she came back faster than the Tasmanian devil and said, 'First one to bed wins a prize.'

I jumped up immediately and ran to the bedroom. I was way better at winning than Tommy. As we ran down the hall, Mum yelled, 'Don't forget to brush your teeth.' I turned into the bathroom like Superman, put the lid of the toilet down and jumped up on it.

Tommy tried to join me on the lid, but I wanted the prize, so I turned into a huge wall and blocked him. Tommy was confused because I'd always let him up, but the race had changed everything. And because neither of us could brush our teeth without looking in the mirror, Tommy just stood there, looking up at me. I smothered my toothbrush in toothpaste, ran it under the water and started brushing, looking down at tiny, confused Tommy, feeling like a god.

'Move over, Trevor.'

'Never.'

'Why?'

'Why do you think, dummy?'

'I'm not a dummy.'

'Kindergarten baby, wash your face in gravy.'

'I'm in grade one,' Tommy said.

'Retard.'

'I'm going to tell Mum.'

'Of course you will, you big fat baby.'

'I'm not a baby.'

'You wet your bed,' I said, 'And so do babies.'

'Shut up or I'll pee in your bed tonight.'

'Before or after you pee yours?'

Tommy was more forceful when he tried to get up again but I outsmarted him. He punched my leg and I absorbed the agony like a super-sponge. When I had my prize, I'd rub it in his stupid face.

'Just let me up.'

'I'm bigger and smarter and faster and stronger and nothing you can ever do will change that.' I looked down from the toilet and watched Tommy turn crayon red. I could see in his eyes how much he wanted to win and how he knew it would never happen as long as I was alive. I towered over him, brushing my teeth fast and then slow and then telling him how I would always beat him at *everything*. His frustration and fury made me so happy. 'Tommy, you're redder than Superman's underwear.'

And he started huffing like a bull in a bullfight. The worse he felt, the bigger I grew. I looked in the mirror and said, 'I wonder what I'm going to win?'

'A punch in the face.'

'Did someone stupid just say something?'

'I'm not stupid Trevvvooor... Let me uuuup.'

'It must be so hard to *always* lose?'

'I hate you.'

'I've never lost anything to anyone ever. I'm invincible.'

'Mum!'

'Keep it down in there. Your brother is asleep,' Mum said.

I stood over him and flexed my muscles.

'Let me up now!'

'What part of *be quiet* don't you understand,' asked Mum.

I leaned down and whispered 'Teeny-weenie cry-baby.' I accidentally spit a bit of toothpaste on Tommy and he screamed.

'Quiet now! Don't make me separate you two!' Mum said.

I leaned over the sink and slowly spit my toothpaste out and watched him squirming. He tried to get up on the lid again but I blocked him with my super-speed. He looked like his head would pop off. I saw a tear. I pointed at it and laughed. I sang 'I'm the greatest, I'm the best.' He froze solid and coiled tightly. Then exploded like a bomb – his arms rushed towards me, his voice rose to a scream and he pushed me with all his might. I was flying, one arm flapping, one still brushing my teeth. I zoomed towards the blue tiles and hoped that they would part like the water in our pool, but they didn't.

—

Even though Tommy and me became best friends again, I knew I had to get revenge. He had tried to murder me and even though the night in the hospital was the best of my life, I had come up with a top-secret super-plan.

I snuck to the bathroom, closed the door and took a pee and then stirred Tommy's toothbrush in the pee-water twenty-two times before putting it back, making sure it didn't touch the other toothbrushes. Waiting to get revenge was even worse than waiting for Christmas; a minute took a day, an hour took a year so it would be seven years before I got him back.

At supper, I watched the clock to make sure it kept moving forward. I was glad I did because it moved backward twice. I asked Mum if we could go to bed early and she made one of her faces and got up from the table and came back with a thermometer and took my temperature. Tommy looked at me like I was Janet-the-Planet. When Mum said my temperature was normal, Dad announced that we could stay up until nine o'clock for the first time ever because we helped him rake leaves.

Tommy yelled YEA!

I don't know what I did but Mum said, 'Trevor, you constantly bug us to stay up late and when we finally let you, you complain?'

The night was so long that I fell asleep on the scratchy shag carpet while watching TV and when Mum woke me up and told me to brush my teeth, I saw that Tommy was gone. I ran to the bathroom and when I saw Tommy standing on the toilet, putting toothpaste on his toothbrush, I said, 'Yes.'

'Yes, what?' asked Tommy.

'Ah... Nothing,' and I dropped my head to hide my bubbly, red-hot face.

Tommy passed me the toothpaste and I wiped it with toilet paper so I didn't get my pee in my mouth. Tommy asked what I was doing and when his face went weird, I realised I was just staring at him like an idiot, so I started to talk and eventually I said there was a hair on the toothpaste.

'Why didn't you just say that?' Tommy said.

I stayed quiet hoping that Tommy believed me because I always threw up whenever I found a hair in a peanut butter sandwich.

Tommy turned to the mirror and moved his toothbrush towards his mouth and as it got close, laughter exploded out of me.

He looked at me and asked, 'What are you laughing at?'

'I'm not laughing.'

'I heard you, stupid. Why are you acting so weird?'

I asked Tommy to move over so I could join him on the toilet. I casually wet my toothbrush. From the corner of my eye, I spied as his toothbrush moved towards his mouth again and I wrestled with my laughing, crushing it, but somehow, just before his toothbrush touched his teeth, an even bigger laugh escaped from me.

'What?' he asked.

'I'm, ah, thinking about something Janet-the-Planet said.'

'I bet it was retarded.'

'Hurry up and I'll tell you when we're in bed.'

I jumped off the toilet and walked around making sure that I didn't *laugh* or say *yes* or do *anything else stupid*. I kept sneaking peeks at Tommy and when he noticed me, I'd look away and hum. I had to be careful because for some reason he was getting suspicious.

When he turned back to the mirror, his toothbrush floated towards his teeth and I squeezed my fists and bit my tongue and it got closer and when the toothbrush finally touched his teeth, I burst with joy and jumped up and down until I heard my voice screaming, 'I peed on your toothbrush!'

Tommy's face crunched up and he screamed, 'Muuuuum!'

Angry footsteps moved towards us.

'I was just kidding, Tommy.'

'Liar.'

Mum stared down at us and asked, 'What in the hell are you two doing?'

'Nothing!'

'Trevor peed on my toothbrush.'

'I'd never say that.'

'Oh, come on Trevor, you just said you were kidding.'

'Stop lying, Tommy.'

'No, you stop.'

'No, you.'

I looked at Mum and felt her X-ray eyes looking through me and then I watched her scan Tommy, who said, 'I wouldn't make that up.'

'No one normal would pee on your toothbrush.'

'You're not normal, Trevor.'

'You're not.'

'I said it first,' Tommy said.

'SHUT UP NOW!' Mum said.

Mum looked at me, then at Tommy, then back to me and because she could read minds, I thought of *me* loading the dishwasher and *me* vacumming and *me* dusting. Tommy started crying like a baby, so I thought of the millions of other good things I'd done and let Mum look into my mind so she could see how pure I was.

I heard a clock ticking like a bomb only really slowly.

And then Mum looked at me and I saw that she believed me. Of course she did. I was the best behaved. I always helped her. I was bigger and better and kinder than Tommy. I was about to suggest a punishment for him when I heard Mum say, 'Switch toothbrushes.'

I said, 'Pardon?'

'You heard Mum,' said Tommy, 'Switch toothbrushes.'

J. Marcelo Borromeo is from the Philippines. At UEA, he was awarded the 2017/18 Seth Donaldson Memorial Bursary. He is working on his first novel, *Residents*, which tells the story of a house that talks to its dwellers and the woman with whom it falls in love: its final inhabitant.

This Must Be The Place
Short story

CHAPTER 1

This is what the house knows:

There was a golf course behind the back wall of the Ramirez residence. Because the only rule Mr Ramirez enforced in his house was to forbid smoking, guests had to climb over and enjoy their cigarettes on country club property, under the shade of a forty-seven-year-old narra tree that leaned heavily to the right.

The sun hadn't risen over the hill of hole 15, and when John checked his watch, he knew that the night wouldn't be over for another half hour. He figured he had enough time to finish his pack of Lucky Strikes. His friends would still be asleep in the basement by the time he was gone.

John heard the flat scratch of slippers on stone and he turned around to see that Ina Ramirez was climbing over the wall to join him.

'Morning,' she said.

'Hey.'

John liked Ina. She was Tim's older sister by five years. John always felt relaxed talking to her, and earlier that night, the two of them decided to hotbox his car. Halfway through a joint, a guard walked by and knocked on their window to ask if they were smoking pot. John said that they weren't, while the joint was still between his fingers, and was prepared to offer a crisp 500-peso note to let them walk. The guard asked if he could take a hit, just to verify, and Ina took advantage by inviting him into the backseat. The guard promised to be quiet and he even shut off his radio, but she started asking him questions about his life in a way that wasn't intrusive.

'How long are your shifts? Do you like your job?'

John could see that she was just trying to make him feel welcome.

She was still wearing the sleeveless shirt from last night, the purple outline of a docile shark tattoo eyeing him from her forearm. But she was also wearing sweatpants, which meant that, at some point during the night, she had decided that this wasn't the sort of house party she needed to dress up for. It was just a get-together for some of her younger brother's dumb friends, and John.

John offered Ina a smoke and she picked it out, leaning in to let him light it with his cigarette. He watched her breathe. He craved conversation.

'When are you flying home?' she asked.

'A little after noon,' John answered.

'How long are you gonna be there?'

'All summer long. Might be back for clearance though.'

'They should have let you just do that before the vacation started. So that you wouldn't have to come back.'

'Yeah, well... I guess they want to wait until grades are out. It'd be weird if you were all set to graduate, and then you find out that you failed something.'

'Oh yeah...' she said, letting her voice fade. She leaned back, looking to the sky. He looked at her. She turned to face him. 'Is it weird for you, having to go back and forth all the time?'

'Not really,' he said. 'I mean, I want to stop moving around. Cebu, I like because it's home. But I like it in Manila because of the people.'

'Really?' she said, smiling. 'You think people *here* are better than in Cebu?'

'Well, I get along with people better.'

'Fair enough,' she said, nodding. 'Maybe one day you'll find the right reason to leave both cities altogether. Maybe you'll even leave the country. I mean, look at me.'

John waited, thinking she would elaborate. But it was needless. He knew what she was talking about.

'When are you supposed to fly out?' he asked.

'Mid-May.'

'Exciting.'

'I guess. I've been to San Francisco a couple of times already, so it doesn't really feel like I'll be going anywhere new.'

'But going back to school must be exciting. Getting to meet so many new people.'

She laughed. 'I should probably tell you that getting a master's is a little different. There's a lot less partying. They're more adult. Think tastings, with cheese and wine.'

'Will you come back when you're done?' he asked.

She took a moment to consider her answer. John thought that maybe she was asking him to read her mind. John knew that people who left the country rarely ever came back. She was going to lead a life that she could never have in the Philippines. It was what she meant when she told him that he needed the right reason to leave. Why go at all if you never dream of staying?

'Maybe,' she finally said. 'If I stayed there, would you come and visit me?'

John could have been coy and repeated her answer back to her. But they weren't close enough to call each other regularly. To adjust to each other's time zones. To keep up. He suddenly felt that after tonight they'd never see each other again.

'Don't go,' he then said. 'Just stay here.'

Ina leaned in and gave him a kiss on the cheek. She waited for him to do something. But he sat unmoving, and slowly she pulled herself up and climbed back over the wall.

John was still watching the wall long after she had disappeared. He was remembering the moment over and over again. He thought of what she said.

In the pack, there were two cigarettes left. He laughed at his failure.

CHAPTER 2

This is what the house knows:

On the night of the opening, there is a modest party. Katerina is meeting most of the people there for the first time. They are mostly potential co-workers, critics from the universities where she's applied to teach.

She chats with one professor, an ageing assistant curator of the Jesuit university gallery who tells her that her work reminds him of Lautrec. Katerina thinks her work is making a good impression. She doesn't jump the gun by talking to him about her intentions.

'If you'd asked to present your work in our gallery, I'm sure we would have been happy to have you,' the professor then says.

'Oh!' Katerina blushes. She could take the opportunity, but she chooses to continue softly. 'I didn't want to presume... I'm only a visitor, and I know the status of your venue is very distinguished.'

'In fact, we've just finished building a new space on campus. It used to be in the old library. It would have been nice to bless the gallery with work from a visiting instructor.'

This is it, Katerina thinks to herself. She isn't slighted by the fact that he said "visiting", but she figures that if there is any moment appropriate for her to press on, this is her chance.

'Yes, my boyfriend Andy spoke very highly of it. Perhaps we can arrange something for when I'm teaching,' she says.

'Yes,' the professor says. 'Wonderful.'

She takes a sip from her glass. She supposes she's done all she could, and considers her labours.

Just earlier that day, she had been worrying over where to put each painting. Up until then, her work had only hung in venues built to function as galleries. Nothing as intimate as this. She gave hours to figuring out what would go in the sala, in the dining room, in the bedrooms, in the bathrooms.

'I was surprised when I first arrived and found that it used to be someone's house,' she says now to the professor.

'The Ramirez family have always been such good patrons. I was surprised when I heard what they had chosen to do with their residence...' His eyes move over her shoulder. 'Have you met the daughter yet? She's the one who runs everything.'

'No,' Katerina says. 'I've only been speaking with her employees.'

'Well, let me have the honour,' he says. 'Miss Ramirez!'

Katerina turns around to see the woman the professor is looking at. She's in her mid-30s, in the middle of admiring one of Katerina's more recent paintings. The woman turns to them with a picturesque smile. Katerina thinks she could very well be the subject of her own painting. Perhaps she already has been, many times over.

The professor steps forward and gently pulls the woman in. 'I'd like to introduce you to our guest,' he says. 'The artist who will hopefully join us this summer.'

'Hello,' the woman says. 'We're so happy to have you.'

'Katerina.'

'Incidentally, I'm called Ina, too.'

Katerina nearly flinches. 'That's a lovely coincidence.'

The professor tries to reinsert himself. 'Ina has been running the gallery since it opened. Before this, she had a stint at the San Francisco MoMA. We were excited to hear that she was giving that up to work back here in Manila.'

'Arturo,' Ina says. 'Don't exaggerate. It was really more on-the-job training. I knew I couldn't stay away from home.'

'You're an *ilustrado* now,' the professor teases.

'I'm curious, Katerina,' Ina says. 'How did you come to hear about our gallery? We're not exactly the first place you'd find on Google.'

'A friend,' Katerina says. She thinks they are going to comment, but they don't, and she decides to be less obscure. 'My boyfriend. He was the one who gave me a list of places to look at when I came over. This place was on the top of his list.'

'Is he here tonight?' Ina asks.

'No. He's in London. He works for a publishing house, and we both agreed it would be better for me to find out how much I'd like Manila without his influence.'

'He's... from Manila?' Ina asks.

'Yes. Well, he used to live in Manila, but his family's from Cebu. I'm to visit them in a few weeks.'

Katerina notices that Ina's lips part and she does not move them, as if failing to speak, to respond.

'And you're planning to move here,' the professor says.

'We both are... But as I said, he wants me to see if I like it here first.'

The professor tries not to pout, but Katerina sees it. She must do something about it.

'From what I've seen,' Katerina says. 'I'm quite pleased. I think I'll fit in just fine.'

CHAPTER 3

Another success, Ina thinks. It's the end of the night. Most of the guests have left, including Katerina. Ina is still wearing her cocktail dress when she goes behind the house to smoke. Now and again, she tells herself it's time to quit.

She looks at the windows of the house she has lived in most of her life. Something has found its way back to Ina tonight, a memory that she thought was hers. But as she looks at each window, she realises that there is so much that this house can keep from her, so much that it can give back with little notice.

She thinks, for instance, about how there is no logic in her explanation for thinking of John tonight. She hasn't thought of him in three years. But tonight there was something Katerina said. Something about a boyfriend who wasn't in Manila, who had a family in Cebu, who had Ina's gallery on the top of his list. Where is John at this time of night? The question is enough to make her imagine life through other eyes.

When Ina moved back, the country club had remodelled the back nine of the golf course, taking down the old narra tree in the process. To climb the wall would mean that she would almost certainly be in the line of fire. She removes her shoes and peeks over. The rough is littered with lost balls. She hesitates.

But it's the middle of the night. She can afford to sit there, thinking secretly of John, and have another smoke or two. She pulls herself over the wall, trying to fathom what the house knows.

This is what the house knows.

This is what the house will always know.

Grace Brown is a former researcher for the House of Lords, where her journalism was featured in *The Times* and *New Statesman*, among others. She is currently completing a short story collection based on the Troubles in Northern Ireland. Her fiction has been published in *Dear Damsels* and *The Weekend Read*. Her story *Hens* was shortlisted for the RSL's V S Pritchett Prize in 2017.

Each Night I Dream Of
Extract from a short story

When my cell door didn't open for exercise hour, I walked to the slit of a window and gazed down at the concrete quad. I observed the women as they mulled to and fro, no bigger than hens, white and speckled, they lurched and wobbled or rested on their bums, as if warming eggs.

It was a prison policy for us to be kept separate from one another. They believed it prevented IRA collusion. I began to pace. The length was smaller than that of a Ford Sierra – my brother's treasured car – with a sleeping mattress less than three inches thick and walls made up of small bricks with ashen grout that crumbled in places and a cell door that stood like a man in armour. Claustrophobic and suffocating. But the thuds of my feet on the floor helped to sterilise my mind. Kept my thoughts shallow and focused my ears away from the sniggers of the rats within the walls. I counted each step. Four thousand two hundred and ninety eight in total. It helped to distract from the pip of loneliness that germinated in my stomach, as the hours locked inside passed from twelve to nineteen to twenty two.

By then I knew that Martha had been right. The blanket protest, our refusal to wear the uniforms they ordered us to, like we were common criminals, had not garnered the result we hope. Instead of reparations, we had been met with punishment. I felt quarantined. First, stripped of our clothes, then stripped of our sunlight. I supposed they thought that would break us.

I continued my paces. The thuds louder with each step. The sun began to set and I was soaked and shivering to the bone. I lay down to rest and woke to pitch-black fog. The darkness of the cell would always surprise me. My eyes adjusted and I made out a splice of moon mirrored on the far wall. A pair of red eyes scuttled below, bright with glee.

The next morning, a message made its way to me: the men had begun their hunger strike, and we were to begin ours. Like the suffragettes before us, we would fight for our cause. I didn't have time to dwell on the limitations of my own mortality. Figured I had stores. Smears of butter spread across my stomach. Thighs creased with crackling. Arms stuffed with crisped chicken skin. The years living off my family's farm had kept me plumped.

There were doubts, of course. Murmurs in my head. How long will it last? What does starvation feel like? But I lacked the experience to invest in them fully. I had felt hunger, the growls of a belly after a long day out fixing fences in the fields, the beat of a headache, staring at revision papers, craving sugar. And despite what people say, no matter how well it is described, to imagine the suffering of others vividly enough to feel it is difficult. Especially in prison. The thick walls numbed your empathy. The darkness displaced your curiosity. Your senses detached with each command to squat during your strip search. Conditioned to think in terms of hours – one hour for breakfast, another for lunch, one and a half for exercise if you deserve it – I couldn't comprehend the expansion of time further than the hour ahead of me.

Six of us signed our bodies up: a housewife, a typist, a single mother, a freshly enrolled student and a linen mill worker. None of us had been taught the extent to which a body deteriorates over time. The pain of a life without sustenance. Without proteins and fat and nutrients. Without smiles and laughs and kisses.

The first week was a ruse. By the fourth day, substantial pangs ping-ponged in my belly and my body was racked with a light-headedness, which shook my focus, and a tickle in my throat left me on the cusp of coughing or throwing up. But I found I could still function. I did my daily paces of my cell. I stretched. Read the books they allowed us to. I made it outside for our weekly exercise.

In the quad, we queued as usual for our turn in the sunlight. The square of yellow folded in on itself as the sun sank back down into the earth. There was no time to dawdle, autumn would evaporate soon and take our patch of warmth with it. There was so much to savour.

Whilst we queued, we regaled each other about our constricted intestines, our parched throats, and heavy limbs. A hand on one another's shoulder, we shuffled towards the patch of delight, muttering words of encouragement and conviction under our breaths. We weren't allowed to fraternise with the other prisoners. They locked us tight together, metal linked like the line of an anchor. We were each other's ball and chain.

'Protect us from the shackles of priest-craft!' Sylvia cried to lift our spirits with her impression of Ian Paisley. 'The breath of Satan is upon us!'

We laughed like vultures.

'Take heart in the fact the Reverend wouldn't last a day in here,' Martha said.

'Far too much lesbian activity,' Sylvia replied.

'You know he's the sort of man who would get off on that secretly,' Ailsa said and we laughed with our heads thrown back. Laughed past the point of sound. Which soothed our throats of their tickle for a moment.

'The man can sniff out a Catholic from a mile off, but God forbid he ever tries to find a clitoris,' said Martha.

I laughed and the gurgles of my stomach did their best to try and draw away my attention. They called for nourishment, sustenance. Laughter, they said, was but empty air.

'Laughter will have to suffice,' I whispered under my breath, as I stepped forward for my turn in the sunlight. Arms spread wide, I breathed the rays into my skin, my lungs, and my heart.

The gurgles of my stomach quieted. I rocked on my heels and felt the creak of my knees, the tightness of my hips. Tinkles of laughter from the other striking women rang in my ears. A thought came to me, breathless in the way the purest truths do: I wouldn't be able to go through this without them. I believed in the cause, in a united Ireland, but that belief was not remedy enough for the pain in my lungs and the spoils in my gut. The kindness of the women picked me up, the sisterhood of their pain drove me. I knew now what was to be my bread and butter, the sprinkle of salt on soup, a hot toddy by a fireplace, feet pointed to the flames. We comforted one another, held each other to account, formed bonds and forged rivers, all whilst rearing families, battling dishes, letting men believe we obeyed them.

I felt a faith rise within me, unfamiliar and ravenous. I was passive in my spirituality. Followed the line at mass for the priest to mark my lips and sipped the blood of Christ and thought of what I'd order from the chippy for dinner. I sinned, gossiped about it to a friend, and then sinned again, harder each time for a greater pleasure. But faith bloomed within me at that moment. My arms lifted higher up to the heavens. I threw out the mumblings of doubts, gnaws of fear.

Behind me, my women carried on their chatter and I felt renewed.

A difficult lesson lay ahead. Renewal was finite. No more than a droplet of fresh water in a salted pan. It drained from me with the new day.

Cramps awoke me from my sleep and cut my body in two. Never had I experienced such an excruciating pain. My intestines curdled. My stomach turned to molten sludge. My liver crystallised, pinning me to the mattress. I folded my knees to my chest, the most movement I could muster. The sun had not risen, but I hoped it would soon. I found it harder to battle pain in the darkness. But the sun would also bring breakfast. Porridge as thick as cement, delivered by the orderly on a rickety trolley, dished out by a ladle, which had to be chewed, and, once swallowed, coagulated to the lining of the stomach. The temptation was unbearable.

Once I thought of the porridge, more images emblazoned my mind: honey-thick toffee sauce poured over a dense but springy sponge, stranded in a pool of corn yellow custard that wafted up a steam of vanilla and sweet milk. Piercing holes in the top of a steak and Guinness pie, rubbing milk onto the uncooked white pastry top, a signal that winter had arrived and fortifications were to be found in the chunks of succulent beef hidden among the generous gravy under the golden lid. A pint of crisp apple cider sipped on the step outside the house, which cleared the tension between the eyes like a cold flannel over a fevered forehead and brought thoughts of trees climbed and school shoes muddied with each burst of taste of apple, as the sun danced over the opposite roofs and painted strokes of pink grapefruit and lemon across the clouds,

I cried out. The cramps amplified. Sweat washed my back. I recoiled from the memories, which were too close and loud, like a swarm of starlings sharing secrets. My tongue roamed my teeth. Perhaps a scrap of bread was lodged between my molars? I pulled my knees closer to my chest and tried to pressurise the pain out of me. Tears travelled down my cheeks and I lapped at them with my tongue, desperate to savour the gloriousness of their salt. I followed the scurry of claws around the edges of the cell. I focused my ears on them rather than the grumble of my stomach, but I found my eyelids begin to drift closed. Consciousness was weakened with each spasm. It should have worried me, that despite no exertion, I found tiredness drove me to sleep more and more each day. God how I longed for a mug of tea: milk, two sugars, and hot enough to scald the throat, strong enough to scrape the enamel from my teeth.

The scurries grew louder. I knew how to trap a rat. My dad had taught me because he thought a girl should know a trick or two. Made from chicken wire, I fashioned the catch mechanism myself so that a door shut behind the beast and locked it in. The chicken wire meant the trap was porous, so I could drop the whole thing in a bucket of water and wait. No need to try and bludgeon the head. Six minutes was long enough for the water to fill their lungs, then I would pull the cage out and throw the carcass on the farm's rubbish heap of broken handles and old wooden boards and ragwort and my brother's ripped woollen jumpers, which he was always catching on fence posts. When the heap was high enough, the farm hands set it alight.

In the cell, I knew I could use my hands. The rats had become brave, careless. My motionless body was another part of the furniture to them. They held court on my knurled knees, pranced across my chest, used my hair as a blanket, and scratched their backs on my collarbone. It wouldn't have been difficult to catch one, and I still had the nail shoved between the loose grout. It would sharpen to a decent point.

The thought of sharpening the file against the stone shot a spark of delight through me. I imagined how the metal would sound against the brick, like my mother's file against her nails, and how the rat would squeal in anguish, as its life loosened from its body. Saliva moistened my dried, blistered tongue. I thought of the violent slashes of the rat's tail as I curled my hands around its neck and twisted, like I used to watch the stable hand do to trampled chickens. How the first bite of silken blood would slicken my throat, and the sinewy muscle would release the weight from my chest, and the lobules of fat would warm my heart. Tremors of pleasure shuddered my body. I fell asleep with my fingers weaved between a tail.

Greg Buchanan was born in England in 1989. Since completing his BA in English Literature at Pembroke College, University of Cambridge, and his PhD at King's College London, Greg has worked on a variety of bestselling, award-winning videogames. He is currently writing *Sixteen Horses*, a literary thriller. Follow him on Twitter @gregbuchanan.

Sixteen Horses

The opening to a novel

Tufts of cloud burned black before the sunrise, the horizon littered with the flotsam of old and rusted silhouettes. They were alone.

'Chemtrails,' the farmer had said to the policeman, early on their walk. Other than this, he had been silent.

And now their torches revealed the edge of a bank, right before the crest of a little stream that cut through the farmer's reclaimed marshland. Along its muddy edge and all around, the reeds sang with flies and crickets, the kaleidoscopic biomass of red and green and blue twitching with every minor wind.

'Where are they?' Alec asked, frowning. It was 5:20AM. He'd left his jacket in the car.

'There weren't any sheep over here,' the farmer said. He leapt over the bank, his boots slipping slightly on the incline. 'They normally love coming over here.'

Alec stared at the mud, and the farmer grinned, his cheeks rosy beneath his dirty white beard. With that thick wax coat and that gut and that voice, the farmer could have been a lunatic Santa Claus. 'You won't fall,' the farmer said. 'Not afraid of a little dirt, are you, Inspector Nichols?'

'No.' Yes. 'I just hope you aren't wasting my time.' This man definitely was. 'And these flies—' Alec swatted one away from his rolled-up sleeve, a great bulbous thing that had nestled on the hairs of his forearm.

'Try covering up next time,' the farmer said. 'Don't know what you expected.'

Alec said nothing.

'If you're worried about the mud, I could get my wife to wash your trousers after, if you like? What waist size are you?'

Alec grimaced. 'Let's just keep going.'

He stepped back, tensing before rushing over the ditch, leaping to the other side and thudding down into the thick and gelatinous mud. He splattered his black trouser legs and the farmer's jeans.

The farmer tutted, smiling. 'Big strong lad like you, afraid of a little mud. What have we come to, eh?'

Alec ignored the remark and tried brushing at the mud around his ankles, but this only seemed to smear it further around the fabric, his palms growing filthy in the process. He wiped them clean against his trouser leg with a grunt.

The farmer walked on. He gestured past a large, half-empty water tank around two hundred feet away, turning to find Alec already on his feet. 'We found them near there.' The farmer's face had fallen.

They continued in silence for a few moments. The sun would soon be there.

He checked his watch. 5.23AM.

'What do you think killed them?' Alec asked.

'I told the girl on the phone,' the farmer said, without looking back.

'You phoned the post office, not me.'

'Well what bloody number was I supposed to phone?' the farmer asked. 'Not my fault you lot share a room with the post office, to be honest.'

'There's an answering machine,' Alec said, quietly.

'Hmph. *Answering machine.*'

They kept on, Alec's question unanswered, the silence drowned out by the buzz of the flies, the distant hellos of scraggly sheep out there in the semi-darkness.

'Harriet's moving out,' the farmer said. 'Did you know?'

'Who?'

The farmer frowned. Another reminder that Alec did not belong.

'Harriet... the lady who lives down the lane,' the farmer said. 'She's moving out, selling up her farm.'

'Oh yes, Harriet....' His tone drifted, struggling for connection. 'I saw the sign.' Alec had driven past it on the way here, a farm twice the size of this one, its animals and land and humans in far better condition. He did not know the name. He knew few out here.

'I'll miss her,' the farmer said. 'They're selling up to live with family, so she says.'

'I think I saw them in town a few times,' Alec said, the pair of them almost at the water tank. 'Were they the ones who made those wagon wheels? They'd mix sausage meat into a kind of – well, kind of cinnamon swirl, I suppose. It's delicious. Used to sell it at their stall. Did you ever try one?' He swatted another fly away from his face.

'No,' the farmer said. 'I'm a vegetarian.'

'Really? My wife tried doing that a few years back, and—'

'No,' the farmer repeated, and the conversation died.

They walked on. The world was still dark, even if only for a little while. The sun was almost free. The day had almost begun.

Fifty feet away, the field gave way to freshly-tilled brown soil, forming mounds everywhere on the uneven earth. Chalky rocks littered the plot in every direction. Every step in this place was as muddy and wet as the last.

Further still, there was a thin wire fence marking the edge of the land, clots of wool decorating it like fairy lights where the sheep had once tried to break through.

But there were no animals in sight now. There was nothing but detritus.

'I don't see what—'

'There,' the farmer interrupted. 'In the ground.'

Alec looked around. For a moment, he could not see a thing but dirt.

'I don't—'

Alec stopped talking, a breeze moving past them both. Something shook along the ground.

He removed his torch and stepped forward, pointing its light at the source. Just three feet away, almost the same colour as the mud itself, there lay a great mound of black hair, coiled in thick and silken spirals.

He moved closer and knelt down. He reached into his pockets, pulled out a pair of latex gloves, and snapped them tight in the cold.

He lifted some of the hair up a little, surprised by the weight of it, at the coarseness. He held it higher and ran his fingers along it, gripping at intervals. Toward the base of the spiral, where the rest of the hair still lay upon the ground, he felt flesh and bone.

Alec put it back where he found it. The sun continued to rise. There was something else.

It was black, almost like plastic in its sheen, a thin half-moon of dulled white at its rim. It looked past him.

There were eyes, large sad eyes in the earth.

Alec stepped back.

'My daughter found them – shouldn't even have been out, I'd grounded her—'

Alec shone his torch across the area. There were others – some close together, some alone... he walked until he was sure he had found the whole set. He paced back and forth, a hundred feet all around.

He counted sixteen submerged heads, all apart, all with only the barest strand of skin on display, all with a single eye left exposed to the sun. One of them had been dug up a little more than the others, revealing the neck, at least. It was unclear how much of the corpse remained beneath the surface.

There were footprints everywhere: his, the farmer's, the daughter's, no doubt... He hadn't been told any of this... he hadn't known...

'Who could do this to a bunch of horses?' the farmer croaked, his eyes blinking. 'Who could make themselves—'

Alec looked up suddenly, acid rising in his throat. The sky was growing brighter, its red spreading like fire, the clouds shifting blue. Still the flies and crickets screamed across the reeds, though nothing crawled along those dead eyes, nothing seemed to touch them.

There was a stone house half a mile away along the horizon.

'Who lives over there?' Alec asked.

'No one.'

Alec stared at it a moment longer. It was a lonely looking place.

'Have you ever seen anything like this?' he asked the farmer. 'It's—'

Grotesque.

Beautiful.

'No. Have you?'

Alec shook his head, stepping back, staring once more at the hair. It was all tails, he could see that now. Piled together.

'That's murder,' the farmer said, his voice soft. 'Just look at them. Look.'

It was in fact a property crime, if a crime had indeed been committed; perhaps animal abuse, trespassing too. If you decide something isn't human, you can do almost anything.

Alec looked at the house again, dark and cold in the distance.

'Do you know anyone who might have a grudge against you? Anyone who might try and cause you harm?'

The farmer tried to smile. 'Apart from my wife? No, no... I get along with folk, always have.' He paused. 'What do I do?'

'We need to get a vet in,' Alec stood up. 'We need to get autopsies performed, if we can. I wouldn't touch them until we know more—'

'Can't afford any of that,' the farmer said.

'You wouldn't have to—'

'And besides,' the farmer interrupted. 'Someone buried them, didn't they? Horses don't just get that way themselves.'

'What about the mud? If this used to be wetland, maybe they... I don't know, maybe they—'

'No,' the farmer said, firmly, without elaboration.

Alec paused, looking back down at the eyes. But for the lack of motion, they might have been alive.

He got his phone out to take some photographs of the scene. They would do until help came. 'Try and keep your other animals away,' Alec said. 'If you can keep your other animals inside or—'

'What about the owner?' asked the farmer.

'Of what?'

'Them – these—' the farmer seemed frustrated.

'What?' Alec glanced down at the heads and up again at this man. 'Were you stabling them?' He paused. 'We'd need to contact the—'

'NO,' the farmer spat. 'No – no – no—'

'Hey, it's OK,' Alec said, stepping closer as the farmer turned away. 'I'm sure it's covered by your insurance.'

'You don't understand – I don't keep horses – I've *never* kept horses.

That's what I tried to tell the girl on the phone—'

A fly landed on the rim of an eye.

'I've never seen these horses before in my life.'

Sixteen horses are found buried on a farm near the sea, with only their eyes exposed to the light of the sun. After Veterinary Forensics expert Cooper Allen travels to the scene and a pathogen is discovered lurking within the fallen animals, the dying seaside community of Ilmarsh goes into quarantine. Across a backdrop of mounting hysteria, disappearances, and an increasingly hostile and cryptic government, Cooper and local Inspector Alec Nichols attempt to uncover the truth behind these shocking events.

Zoe Cook was the recipient of UEA's David Higham Scholarship. She grew up in Lincoln and moved to Sheffield to study for her BA and MA in Creative Writing before pursuing this MFA. Her flash fiction has been published in several eclectic online literary journals. Her first novel, *Violet*, explores a thrilling and devastating friendship between two teenage girls and the everlasting havoc they wreak upon each other.

Violet
Extract from a novel

I had never been to a funeral before. Well, I didn't officially attend. But I was there. I didn't think most people my age had been to one before either. The rumour was that Jacob's parents had gone out of town to find a suitable coffin for him.

It was a windy, wintery day. Mr and Mrs Rogers had had to delay the funeral. They had to wait a few months to get their son's body back from the police. From where I was, I could see it was windy enough for women's hats to fly off and into the face of someone else and the candles they were all carrying kept blowing out. I couldn't spot my parents, though they'd told me they were going. I thought it was unusual for them to go, considering the circumstance. My mother had clattered into my bedroom that morning, walking funny in new shoes, her black coat belted tightly around her, to inform me that they were attending the funeral. I was told to stay put.

But I couldn't just stay put. It had been four months since I'd seen you and I had no idea where you were but I had some secret hope, a crazy wish that you might be there, peeking from the trees, just to watch the chaos you had left behind.

The graveyard was dull and brownish. Flatness stretched out for a good mile. It was the only one in town. As I stood still, watching from the back, I could feel the rumblings in the ground from the nearby train station.

There were kids from my school and some from the other, better school and I wondered what the hell they were doing there. Girls with long hair, girls with short dresses despite the weather, the type of girls who wouldn't look twice at Jacob but had fallen in love with his death, were holding onto the walls of the church and crying somewhat hysterically. Everyone was standing outside, shivering in the cold waiting for the family to show up. I was waiting too.

A long black limo drove in. I ducked my face as it passed me by. Everyone turned to watch. The driver had trouble navigating the uneven paths and almost ran over a grave and everyone held their breath. Mr Rogers and Jacob's little brother, Dean, got out first. The car door was left open but nobody else appeared. Then Mr Rogers leant down and said something, it looked like he was shouting. Out came Mrs Rogers. She had a black dress on and no coat. I thought the dress was too tight on her. Dean held out his little hand but she ignored him. Mrs Rogers looked to be ignoring most people. She just stared ahead, right into the mouth of the church, the spot at the front where her son was lying dead in a coffin, waiting to be put in the earth. I wondered if she was picturing Jacob the way I saw him, lying on the floor and clutching uselessly at the hole in his stomach, his eyes emptying, right as cars glided past on the street outside.

Everyone moved into the church. I scanned the field around me. It was empty. Leaves shivered from trees and that was about all there was. I slumped with disappointment. I wasn't thinking about Jacob lying so still, all dressed up in his best suit, his lips pinched white, though maybe I should have been. As always, I just wanted you.

Badly-sung hymns swelled from the church, the type of shit Jacob would have hated, let's be honest, and there was a point at the end of the song when some people finished before others and then everything fell flat.

Frank Costello was born in London in 1994. He graduated with a First in Philosophy from New College of the Humanities in 2015. He is an ex-world pool champion (under 18), a Royal Academy exhibited artist, and the recipient of UEA's Kowitz Scholarship. He is working on a novel set in contemporary London, about a teenage drug dealer whose friend has been stabbed.

High Rising
Novel Extract

Jamie James shuffles from Nike to Nike at the foot of Mousc's block, ears on the intercom's steady bleep, hands clenched in trackie-bottom pockets along with keys, wallet, iPhone, chunky Nokia, drawstring purse containing ⅜ of tightly packed weed, and a slim wad of cash. He unclips and removes the massive, bright blue bike helmet he shares with Mouse from his normal sized head – Mouse's head is roughly twice as big as your average man's – tucks it between his arm and side, lifts his hood up, and stuffs his hands back down. The helmet's really not his style. Nor's the high-vis vest – also shared with Mouse – dangling down him like a dress. But they're not worn for aesthetic reasons. Nor for the safety considerations your average law-abiding citizen goes in for. Only reason Jamie's sporting such incredibly uncool, unflattering apparel is he and Mouse are in the know: the police never suspect a man in proper bike attire.

Jamie and Mouse go way back, first meeting when Mouse joined Jamie's primary school in year 3. This was after Mouse got expelled from his previous school for teasing a loose brick out of the playground wall one morning and launching it at this big nasty kid – Mouse himself was very small back then, the hulk-like transformation puberty would bring still a few years off – who was always doing your standard, fairly low-key, primary-school-bully type stuff to him like pushing his head into the drinking fountain tap and stealing his juice carton; the force with which the brick struck the other kid's big nasty head leaving him with severe, piss-your-pants, can't-remember-your-own-name style brain damage. At least that's the story Jamie got from the school's rumour mill at the time. He's never tried to confirm with Mouse just how true it is. What would be the point? Mouse really isn't one for dwelling in the past much.

Jamie glances up along the block's dirty-grey length and freshly clocks something he's clocked many times before: this old block – the block where Mouse first crawled, took his first steps, said his first words etc. – has the blank, looming presence of a bouncer stood outside a club. Silent. Muscular. Unmoving. Staring off into the middle-distance. Very much Not To Be Fucked With.

Jamie's opinion about Mouse's seeming lack of concern regarding the brick-throwing and other what-you-might-think-were-fairly-major life events can go one of two ways. When he's recently witnessed Mouse saying or doing something that strikes him as especially dumb, he's likely to conclude it's indicative of Mouse having some pretty serious mental deficiencies of his own, his lifelong academic record giving weight to this reading. However, at other times – most of the time – he's liable to draw a quite different, more generous conclusion. This being that it's actually really quite healthy, this extremely unconcerned way of being Mouse has, that we could all even learn a thing or two from it about how not to waste time pointlessly dwelling in the past. There's something almost sage-like about it, he thinks, when feeling particularly charitable towards his old pal, like the outlook of a committed Buddhist or top-drawer athlete. Jamie's reflective enough to realise there might be some self-interested reasons he's drawn to this conclusion (who wouldn't prefer not to see the guy you spend the vast majority of your free time with as just another imbecile, oblivious and occasionally extremely violent, but instead as someone who's different in an interesting and cool way, as a guy with some hidden profoundness, as a dude basically living in a permanent state of spiritual enlightenment?), but he also has daily evidence – a perceptive comment here, an appropriately wry smile there – that there's more to it than this, that he actually does intuit more than first meets the eye in his very large, very uneducated friend.

This rapid left-to-right shuffle of Jamie's shuffling makes him resemble a man standing on hot coals but its actual purpose is more the opposite: not to freeze out here, in this real granny-killer of a winter's evening.

'Come on, come on, come on,' he says, his words turning white before him. He pictures Mouse getting up off the sofa, walking down the hallway, buzzing him in – hoping against hope thinking will make it so. But then a wave of wind whistles around the block and hits him side-on and hard and his picturing's disrupted and he narrowly avoids a topple and his hood's caught and left flapping behind him like the wing of a startled pigeon. Nights this cold cause the constant prioritisation of some body parts over others and it's his hands he now favours – he keeps them safely stowed in the shelter of his trackie-Bs and begins flinging his head back in an attempt to re-hood without them. This movement gives him a new look: that of someone angrily reacting to being either spat or bird-shat on, both of which happen on this particular South London council estate – the estate Jamie also lives on, in a near-identical block not a minute's walk from here – about as frequently as one would expect from an estate that looks like this one.

Plus, what confirms the deep-down-he's-a-genius narrative Jamie tends to favour with regards to Mouse is the seemingly endless street smarts the guy exhibits. Like Jamie could see how a fella like him – one who's from the age of thirteen been well known on the estate as Not To Be Fucked With – could easily end up with little respect for the world's dangers. But no, it was Mouse who'd first suggested they don the fluorescent vest and helmet when on bike and carrying. And it was Mouse who'd planned and designed this nifty mechanism that, if they were to end up in a sticky situation with the police, would allow them to force whatever they were holding out of a little hole in their pocket so that, thanks to an old-fashioned, drawstring purse and a small piece of string, it would dangle down around where one's manhood dangles and so would be passed over by the stop-and-searcher as either nothing or – if they proved to be the kind of stop-and-searching guy or gal who likes to cop a feel – nothing but eyebrow-raisingly impressive. And, perhaps most hidden-genius-narrative confirming of all, it was Mouse who'd had the idea of making money on the side as they do in the first place – of buying in bulk online and then specifically and solely selling to the young, middle-class crowd that, thanks to Jamie's academic success (and resulting private school scholarship) they had easy links with, since they were a) harmless, b) loaded, and c) even more scared of getting into shit with the police than he and Jamie were. Jamie's aware that a real argument could be made then, that – contrary to what unknowing outsiders might think – Mouse is really not the Lenny to his George, the Pinky to his Brain, but is in fact the real mastermind behind their whole operation, the truly talented thinker in the pair, the one you might just want to watch out for in the future – but Jamie's sure as hell not going to be the one to make it.

Jamie abandons his backwards-head-flinging after the third or fourth unsuccessful fling and re-hoods with a bare, now wind-exposed, left hand. He feels it begin to move from painfully numb to a more worrying, painless stage as another gust bites icy around the block and wishes a range of terrible possible futures on his friend twelve floors up. He then cups and blows hard into it and quickly re-pockets it as his eyes and head follow this new hot white exhalation up along the length of concrete until it's gone into the smudged-chalkboard sky above. All is still, now, but for his general slight shiver and loud-chattering teeth. The intercom's bleep continues unanswered. He thinks of Mouse once again, pictures him in his flat way up there, in its lazy warmth, bum glued to the sofa, eyes to his laptop, getting more and more stoned with each passing YouTube clip without him. *Let me in, you bastard*, he thinks. With his head tilted right back it's almost like the block's beneath his feet, like he could just walk on up it, walk up all twelve floors, the world ninety degrees off from the norm, looking in windows as he does. He imagines doing this, imagines using it like a pier going out to sky, imagines looking down and in from it, down and in on Mouse as he blazes away, before opening up a window to drop through, lighting up beside him, joining him once more in that familiar land of mindless comfort. 'Lean', they call it, that couched state of highness that comes on when you're a few strong spliffs in. The kind of high where movement never seemed so hard, like where you run a cost-benefit analysis between walking to the toilet and pissing your pants right there on the sofa and it comes out as a dead heat, tied. Satisfaction's ghost runs through him as he thinks of it. He closes his eyes. He longs for it. Oh, to be lean and warm. He wonders how long it'll be before one of his fingers just drops right off.

The intercom's bleep becomes a faint crackle but Mouse's deep, yawning voice doesn't come through.

'Mate, it's me,' Jamie says into the speaker, waiting to hear that heavy, sweet, slowness that enters his friend's tone whenever he's nicely lean, like a voice box drenched in honey. 'Buzz me in willya?'

Just his expectation's enough to get a bulb of envy glowing within; but he stands and waits and there's nothing but staticky word-fragments in response – it's like he's halfway between two radio stations, like he's been rung by someone's arse. A couple of possible explanations spring to in his head. The first being that Mouse is fucking with him, that this is some dumb prank he's playing, one with an imminent, shitty punchline. And going on past form he knows that's more than possible. The other's that the intercom's just playing up, gone on the blink again, as it's also prone to do.

'Will you please just buzz me—'

Two words, real distorted, stop him mid-sentence.

'Fuckin help,' is what he thinks he hears it crackle.

He strains his ears but the buzzing the door makes when unlocked via intercom then starts up; there's no longer that faint, bowl-of-Rice-Krispies sound you get when there's someone on the other end.

'Mouse? Mouse?'

There's nothing but the buzz.

Jamie's heart rate escalates, images of gore/handcuffs passing through his mind's eye. But then he stops and thinks for a moment, decides Mouse was probably just saying 'Fuckin hell.'

Deep breath. No need to panic. Glitchy intercom it is.

Emily Coutts is a writer and teacher who lives in Norwich. She is currently working on two projects: *Double History*, a dark comedy about historical sexual abuse in boarding schools, and a collection of short stories that all feature the same psychotherapist and her daughter.

The Long Way Around
A Story

The council are building a bypass around my hometown. It is a Saturday, the day when I should be marking essays or looking after my non-existent children, but instead I am sitting in a long line of traffic on the road to my parents' house. From here I can't see the bypass for what it really is, or what it is going to be. I just see a ditch in the ground and a lot of men in hard white hats, breathing hard white breaths into the cold. I also see machines, which are fearsome and inexplicable, but then I have to concentrate on the road ahead.

When I arrive home my father watches me park and says, 'Well done for not hitting the wall this time,' and I smile, because the red mark from my car is still on the wall, and the white mark from the wall is still on my car. My father hugs me and says, 'How are you?' in a voice that implies he already knows the answer. My mother has baked.

We eat homemade soup and stilton. I want to thaw out here at the table with my parents – their predictable love – but after eight years in a career I can't stand I have reached an end of some kind, and my father does not believe in such endings. A silence settles as we cut my mother's cake, which is delicious and still a little warm.

After lunch she says, 'I have a client at 3 and I need to look at my notes,' which is her way of saying, 'You two need to talk about this between yourselves.' But my father is busy completing a Sudoku under timed conditions, and nothing registers.

'Dad, shall we go for a walk?' I ask.

He doesn't look up from his puzzle.

'Robert,' says my mother.

'Yes.' His eyes are still down.

My father completes his Sudoku in 23 minutes, 15 seconds, which is 6 minutes, 45 seconds less time than the *Saturday Times* says it should take.

'Good to know your old dad's not a complete dotard yet,' he says. He puts on the older of his two green wax jackets. I wore it once to do the gardening. It smelled of old apples and leaves.

'Darling, you look thoroughly disreputable,' says my mother, heading upstairs to her counselling room with two glasses of water. 'We must get you a new coat.'

'This one's got years in it,' says my father, quickly, because he dislikes anything new on principle.

As we head out, my parents' front door closes with its familiar shudder, and the key makes the exact noise it always makes in the lock.

'Long walk or medium?' asks my father.

'Long.'

'Good. I want to show you the bypass.'

As we walk down the street, I see the things I've never not seen: the unchanged houses, the same large field across the road. Even the leaves disintegrating in the gutters seem everlasting. When I was a little girl, I used the trees on that field as wide-spaced football goals and stole their conkers and hid them in a special drawer. When I think of home, it is always autumn.

My father tells me about the bypass, about the pile drivers and the diggers, the lorries that come in the night and wake him up. 'Old Micky Flanagan's been naysaying it in the paper,' he says. He means the local newspaper, not the *Times*. 'But he's the godfather of all grumpy old men.'

I don't trust myself to reply to this.

'How are you?' he says again.

'I'm fine.' If I were with my mother she would hear the silent 'so there' at the end of this, and the soundless 'help me' beneath it. But I am on a walk with my father, so he talks about the bypass instead.

'I've been saying we need this road since 1997,' he says. It's colder now we're leaving the houses behind, and I shiver a little. My father digs into a torn pocket and produces a tweed hat, the sort that people from the city think all people from the countryside wear. I put it on, hoping that nobody I used to know is still around to see.

'It suits you,' says my dad. 'Are women wearing flat caps these days?'

'Not that I know of.'

'Your mother's highly amused that beards are back in fashion. She thinks I'm going to shave mine off in protest.'

'That seems like the sort of thing you'd do.'

'No. I couldn't do without the beard. I'll just have to grin and bear it until they become embarrassing again.'

'Sounds like a wise course of action.'

We walk on in silence. We're nearing what will be the bypass now, passing people sitting in the endless traffic jam. My father knows one of the drivers, someone he used to teach, and they wave to one another. He glances down at the Fitbit on his wrist.

'Only 8,000 so far today,' he says. According to government guidelines the average adult needs to walk 10,000 steps per day to avoid cardiovascular disease, but my father always exceeds 12,000.

We arrive at our destination.

'Ta da,' says my father, without enough irony. 'They're really making progress with the embankments now.'

We stand and stare at rubble, at bent wire fences and craters and earth. I try to imagine the bypass through my father's eyes: the trucks and the diggers and the workmen like toys spread out on a carpet sixty years ago, in front of a little boy. But all I can focus on is the ground, which is churned up and pocked with copper-coloured puddles.

'They nearly hit a pipeline in September but it's back on track now. Look at that crane.'

I look. It is stringed with suspension wires and rotating through the freezing air.

'It's a fascinating process,' he says. 'They're already £50,000 over budget, though. The planning permission alone took months because of the conservationists, and now it's too cold to dig the drainage. They won't lay the foundations until at least March, and that's the good bit. First, they'll pack down the sand and the dry earth, then the rubble and the cement, then the bitumen goes on top. It'll be good to clear the town of all this traffic.'

'Dad, I hate my life,' I say.

When my father was a little boy, he lived in a large house in the countryside. His father spent all his free time doing the garden and his mother hid the gas bills in the bread bin.

'Oh,' he says.

'I don't really know what to do about it.'

My father gives me another hug. He smells of old apples and leaves.

'That job. We are so proud of you.'

'I know.'

'Your mum said you're finding it tough but I bet you're brilliant. And the kids love you, of course they do.'

'The adults don't.'

'Well, no one likes being told what to do, do they? Least of all you.'

He smiles at me but I can't smile back. There is a pause. I watch a truck upend a crate full of earth.

'The only place I like in that school is the toilet,' I say.

'What?'

I can't cry in front of my father but I've learned that I can tell him about the crying.

'When I'm in that toilet I don't have to pretend to be anybody. Yesterday I cried in there and then I couldn't stop.'

Before my father was a little boy, his father was sent to war. When my father's father came home he was too poor to become a gardener, so he had to become a teacher instead.

'I'm sorry that's how you feel,' says my father, nodding to himself. It is a too-subtle thing for him to say, so I guess that my mother has taught him how to say it.

My father's father retired early from teaching with a mental breakdown, which he called 'just a spot of nerves'. He didn't understand those sorts of things.

My father and I watch as work on the bypass comes to a standstill. The men in hard white hats share tea from a thermos. Hot air lifts off the cups like fog. Behind them, the crane looks menacing, as if it might start to move on its own. I shiver again.

'You're cold,' says my father. 'Shall we go back the long way around?'

The walk home takes us right out into the Fen. Empty fields stretch for miles before us, hard and unrelenting.

'My worry is that you'll leave teaching and just feel even worse.'

When I was a little girl, my father kept a spreadsheet totalling all our household expenditure. My mother suggested she train as a counsellor; my father made a face. He came back from work every evening with his black briefcase, and he only sometimes had a headache.

I think about the old song that I've been listening to on repeat for months. It's called *Imitation of Life*. Sometimes on my way to work I walk down the wrong street just so I can hear the song again. In the evenings I lie in my bed and wait for it to be time to go to sleep.

'I'm not sure it's possible to feel worse, Dad.'

'But what else is there to do?'

'I can't know that yet. Travel, maybe, and live. I could go back to uni.'

'In my day you went to university and then you went to work. There's no point in all this endless education. And what about the money?'

'There are loans,' I say. 'And I've been saving.'

When my brother left home, my father couldn't account for 53p in the household spreadsheet, and he refused to come down to lunch. He woke up crying every morning for six months. I told him not to worry – he'd probably just bought a Mars bar and forgotten about it.

'I've never been in debt in my life,' he says.

'Yes. And you had free grammar schools and a government that paid you to go to university and house prices 85 times cheaper than they are now accounting for inflation,' I say, because I was raised by my father.

'Fair point,' he says, and smiles.

We walk on. At length the path curves and we start to head back towards the town, leaving the barren fields behind us. My body's warm from walking, but my fingers feel numb. I make fists in my pockets.

A thought occurs to me. 'Dad,' I say. 'What do you do when you're sad?'

'I never really know I'm sad because I'm too busy being in the feeling. I get a headache and decide I've got brain cancer, and then I lose my appetite. Your mother usually has to tell me what's going on.'

When my father had a mental breakdown, my mother sent him to the vicar, who sent him to the counsellor, who sent him to the doctor. Afterwards my father suggested my mother train as a counsellor; my mother made a face.

'When I'm sad I don't have anyone to tell me what's going on,' I say, 'because I'm on my own.' I can't cry in front of my father, but sometimes I wish that I could.

'You have us,' he says. 'You'll always have us.'

When we get back to our street, the horse chestnuts look even barer than they did when we left. We walk down the same pavement with leaf mulch sticking to our shoes. Once we get inside I will drink tea with my mother, but my father believes that hot drinks are inefficient, so he will sit down in his usual spot on the sofa and complete a Sudoku under timed conditions. And I will feel one deep, pure, heartbeat of grief, because for a minute there we were talking.

Jill Crawford is the John Boyne Scholar at UEA. Fiction in *The Stinging Fly* and *n+1*; forthcoming in Faber's anthology *Being Various: New Irish Short Stories*. Non-fiction in *Boundless (Unbound)*. Jill was an actor. She is writing a Northern Irish *Künstlerroman*. Represented by Karolina Sutton in London and Anna Stein in New York.

A European
Extract from a novel

She was first to arrive at the macaron shop. Though the café was not full, she took a table under the awning on the street. It was drizzling. She was wearing a flimsy dress and sandals, and had neither coat nor umbrella, but she did have her sunglasses – of course, no use in the circumstances. She mulled over which flavour to choose, just the one, and watched tourists gather at the entrance of the shop to take photos. There was nothing to stop a car from careening off the road into them.

She'd seen this same shop elsewhere in Manhattan, all over, if not *yet* in Belfast. Why would you take a picture of yourself outside a shop that's everywhere? This one wasn't even that picturesque. People are mugs, she concluded, as she often concluded about people.

While waiting for Tam to arrive, as arranged, outside the macaron shop on Madison Avenue, less than a day after the latest atrocity, she glanced again at his Tinder profile. She hoped he would look like his photos. They were good, authoritative and seductive, apart from the magazine cover in which he appeared in full combat apparel above the headline MODERN AMERICAN SOLDIER, like a GI Joe manikin, a manoeuvrable doll. He was eight years older than her if he was telling the truth. He seemed to carry his experience lightly, incredibly so.

She sat there for ten, fifteen minutes, during which time several cars dashed past – or was it the same car several times? – with horns screaming and 'Free Palestine' banners flying from open windows. Families with blue and white flags passed down the street. She hated flags, all of them. The parade must have finished. It was 3:20 in the afternoon.

In their final Tinder exchange the evening before, Tam had written:
Do you burn or do you like the sun?
I prefer to stay pale, she'd replied. *I like to be all one colour.*
Oh, I see.
You prefer tanned, like you?
Not particularly. There's a chance that tomorrow may make it to a rooftop pool...
Love swimming but not on a first date.
Kay kay. Not sure what we can do that will preserve your porcelain skin but would like to do something with you.

I have a sun hat. What's your schedule?
A sun hat wasn't required today.

Tam arrived, at last, in his cargo shorts with his great calves. He was silvering fair, candid blue, had a hint of a paunch. He looked like a kind of human lion. They shook hands and he apologised for taking a while, offered to get drinks. She'd take a decaf latte and a pineapple macaron.

He went inside and she looked through the window, slyly. Here was a man in the simpler sense, wholly sure of himself, a man who could chop down a tree. He was unlike anyone she'd ever dated. She was surprised at how attractive he was, at how primitive she must be. He wasn't carrying a gun; there was nowhere to conceal it. Anyway, she'd decided to park her political views. She didn't want to think ethically today. If they could go somewhere and no talking because she didn't need to get to know, to feel the burden of that. She might never tell anyone about this.

Once, Benji had got her lost on the way to a macaron shop. She'd wanted to buy a gift before catching a train she then nearly missed. They had squabbled and he had stomped off, and she'd called him a scatty mean dude to leave her in the middle of a strange city like that, with an unwieldy case.

Tam returned with the macaron and a chocolate éclair, half of which he offered after she had polished off hers without offering.

– Oops, she said. No thanks. I'm a bit of a purist. Tend to like one thing or the other. They smiled, both thinking perhaps that she must be the opposite of him.

– Mary's a chocolate addict, he said.

– Is that right? His wife was Mary then. Do you do this a lot?

– Always have. He looked amused, delighted. Have you?

– No, I've never done this. I'm not a *unicorn*, I don't think. She'd done quotes in the air. Why had she done that? She strongly disliked them.

– Are ya *sure*? He mimicked the gesture.

– More of a mole or a hedgehog. I'm just curious.

– Curious is good. We can work with curious. His parents were lawyers. His sister was a deputy mayor. No children. No way, he said. Mary got tempted a while back and now we've a rabbit called Stump.

– Stump?

– It's got one leg and a stump.

– How does it hop?

– Terribly, but he doesn't know any different. You any pets?

– I'm only here for a bit, looking after somebody's place while they're away. I live in London.

– London's cool.

– I'm sick of it.

– We had an actress move in with us once, he said. Our girlfriend. She was great. We were happy for like a year until she told her parents. They're Catholic.

– Oh dear.

– Yep. They said she was a freak, living with freaks, giving up a chance to have a husband, kid, normal life, la la la. She moved out. We'd have married her, but we're already married to each other, so no can do.

– That's a shame.

– She went back to her scumbag ex. Hope her folks are happy now.

– Was it a serious thing?

– Yeah, we loved her. Mary was even more into her than I was.

– Ha, you felt left out.

– Not really.

– Does your family know you and Mary are?

– Open? Sure. Everyone does. My sister set us up. She met Mary at a corporate gala and was like: Who is this hot, skinny, free-thinking redhead that's into guns? My brother's gotta meet her.

– Nice sister.

– Nah, my sister's a bitch. She's bitter because she's fat. You married?

– It was a mistake.

– Why?

– He was. Um. I. He.

– Lucky escape, then.

– Yup. She gulped quietly.

– No kids?

– Huh. No.

– What are you doing after this?

– Heading downtown to do a scratch of a new play, as a favour for a friend.

– Where?

– Basement of a pub.

– A British pub?

– Doubt it. There's no such thing.

– What's the play about?

– Fictitious Capital.

– Fancy.

– It's funny. She's funny, my friend.

– You wanna grab a drink first, with me and Mary?

– It might be weird.

– Nah, she'll like you.

– OK. I suppose there's no reason why not.

– That's the spirit. Lemme call.

As he spoke to Mary, she took out her phone, checked her emails, texts: nothing.

– You dropped your mobile, he said.

– This morning. So dumb. It flew out of my hand when an old lady bulldozed into me in the line for the bus.

– Oh, man.

– She was rude. At home, people queue. Anyway, I can't send it off to get fixed. I don't know my way around yet without Google Maps. She rubbed together her finger and thumb. Specks of the cracked screen had dug into the skin. Her fingertips tingled, seared.

– Lemme look. He took the phone. Who's that?

– It's a dancer.

– You like to dance?

– When I'm drunk.

– We're on a cleanse. No booze for three months.

– Why? Don't you think a certain amount of drinking eases life along? As they were chatting, a boy came up too close to her while peering into the shop window to better view the display, bewitched by its arrangement of macaron pyramids in lush botanical shades: greens, blues, amber, coral, coconut. Instinctively, she tilted away from the boy towards the glass, kept talking.

He frowned, paused, roared at the boy.

– Hey! Step away from her! Give the lady her space!

Leaning forward, he reached out and pushed the boy back quite firmly, with a big stern hand against the narrow breastbone. The boy flinched, twisted, jerked into the pavement, bumping into his mother, who stood hand in hand with a little girl. The girl toppled off the kerb into the road. A motorbike swerved wide and the rider wailed something over his shoulder, propelling on. The mother regained her footing, lunged down to snatch the child, and pulled her up to relative safety.

– Jeez, no manners, Tam growled.

The mother threw them a jarring white-hot look but didn't speak. Her lips slightly opened and a thin moan sounded. The family fumbled off in the direction they'd come.

Aud had jumped when Tam had shouted, jogging the slight metal table and dashing her drink. Taupe slush had skited across the surface. Tinged foam clung to the flanks of the cup. Her hand had leapt to her mouth, was still at her mouth, holding feeling at bay. Tam turned, frowning.

– Keep your hair on, she said. He was just a kid.

– Vermin, he replied. His eyes were low. They didn't yield.

– Yeah, vermin, she agreed, without at first knowing why. Tam reminded her of someone. He reminded her of someone who'd hooked his fingers about her throat and crushed, who'd pushed in rigid alien things, who'd sought dominion over her body, who'd tried to gouge and pluck the good out of her, whose eyes had rattled with pleasure as he delved, gnawed. Those eyes were known to her. They were not Benji's eyes, but sometimes Benji had looked through those eyes. They were pitiless and deserted and needy, all at the same time. She felt sick. Her legs prickled. Her toes were stiff and lurid pink. I'm chilly, she said.

They left the café, walked east on 70th street past the Asia Society, and down Lexington to the subway at 68th by Hunter College. At the ticket barrier onto the platform, her MetroCard beeped; she was out of juice. He leant back and swiped his card a second time to let her through.

– Thanks, she said, I'll pay you back next time. The mother's face remained with her, burrowed in. What if the child had fallen into traffic? What if the bike hadn't swerved? What if that small life had been snapped right there in front of them?

In the carriage of the train, he stood close. He was solid and she felt like gas. He was so at ease as he eyed her. He was only interested in what he could do with her flesh. He didn't hide it. The eyes pressed. She wanted them.

Rain was heavy when they came out of Penn Station. He didn't seem to mind. They ducked into a pharmacy. Umbrellas were arranged in a stand by the door, black and squat and at twenty dollars a rip-off. She bought one, sausaged in cellophane, and broke it open with her teeth.

People sheltered beneath the lips of buildings, under liquefying scaffolds. The city dripped, stank. A breeze came and went. Her feet slipped in her sandals, slime and grit between the toes. She nearly fell. He caught her arm, and held it. He had her. She needed to be there. The pressure felt right. Her skin burned a bit.

As they approached the park, he told her about his advocacy work for a state-of-the-art gun silencer. He was an entrepreneur.

– I've a design shop in Queens, where we build and customise fire arms, armour.

– What for?

– Personal use, TV, film stunts.

– TV?

– *Boardwalk Empire*, *Daredevil*, *Orange is the New Black*. Heard of any of them? He winked.

– No. She couldn't bring herself to smile.

– There's an auction next week. They're selling the last fragments of steel from the rubble of the Twin Towers. I was actually a first responder.

– God.

– Yeah. The larger pieces have gone to museums, memorials, to build a warship, etcetera. So I'm working with a guy, who'll bid for the final few shards. Plan is we melt them down and make a select number of bespoke handguns, ideally 9mm, and ideally eleven of them.

– Wait, you want to make guns out of.

– And bullets, too. We're gonna inscribe the guns, really beautifully, with the date.

– The date? Oh. Wow.

– It's a frickin awesome idea. People are gonna eat it up.

SEAN DAVID GILBERT

Sean David Gilbert is a former event producer and freelance journalist now working in fiction. His non-fiction has appeared in a variety of zines and magazines (*Time Out*, *The Metro*, *The Holborn*) and he holds a degree in English from Cambridge University. His short fiction focuses on encounters between strangers, and he is currently writing a novel.

The Atrocity Hotel
Extract from a short story

At some point, flying over Austria, or possibly Slovenia, she turned forty. As her plane taxied at Tuzla International, Sarah regained reception and the first trickle of messages delivered. Something about birthdays made serious people turn mystic. She skimmed two texts, which referred to her 'path' and 'the road ahead' and 'fortune', then switched off her phone.

Border control was a teenage boy standing behind a gilded rope; he seemed surprised by the influx of travellers, as if the plane had shown up unannounced and he had no method for sorting through them. Sarah waited on the tarmac as fellow passengers gathered, listening to the steady murmur of complaints. They were all unintelligible and the sound was oddly ambient. At first, she tried to pick apart the languages – Bosnian, Croat – then gave up and floated in the noise.

By one a.m., Sarah was in the car park. She was to travel to Sarajevo by minibus, a three-hour journey, where she would check into a hotel for the night, before starting her story the next day. The uniformed driver stood smoking by a kiosk and when Sarah presented her ticket he turned it left and right, its meaning apparently indecipherable. He returned the paper and folded his arms, appearing keen to forget about the whole business. Sarah stood next to him, making sure he couldn't leave without her, and waited. Together, they watched passengers drift from the airport. Sometimes, when standing in a foreign airport late at night, Sarah felt like an anthropologist, examining a divergent, more primitive strain of humanity. At times like this, however, her own humanity felt questionable. London faded from her mind and she faded with it; she had the sense that if she screamed, nobody would turn their head.

Without thinking, she switched on her phone and was immediately alerted to two missed calls from Jeremy. She'd forgotten to tell him that she was leaving, only sending a message on her way to Heathrow. Within minutes, he rang; it was as if he could see her, see his window of opportunity.

'I got your email,' Jeremy said. His voice was stern.

'Sorry, I know this is last minute. I had to take the story.' 'Had to.'

'I thought I'd mentioned this... The article on tourism in Bosnia?''Oh, a piece on tourism! Didn't know they moved you to breaking news.''OK I *wanted* to work. You know how I get around birthdays.''Yeah... It's just, I'd gotten us a table at the Chiltern Firehouse, as a surprise.' Sometimes he was like a puppy, dropping strange gifts at her feet. She had no idea what to do with them.

'That place is horrendous,' she said.

He laughed. '*The Standard* describes it as a "celebrity haunt". Apparently, the cast of *Made in Chelsea* can be seen at the bar "quaffing champagne until the early hours".''You understand I'm turning forty.'

'I understand that... nobody is too old for celeb spotting.''I don't think they count as celebrities.''Snob. So I... Oo.. tt...ee...some time.' A failing signal cut apart Jeremy's remark. From the tone of his voice, Sarah assumed he had made a joke and so she laughed non-committally. She hated making people repeat themselves.

'Did you hear what I just said?' he asked.

'Yes.''Then why are you laughing?''Perhaps I misunderstood... You're very quiet.'The bus driver abruptly woke from his stupor and began herding people towards his vehicle.

'I looked at flight prices,' Jeremy said. 'I could come and meet you.''That's a bad idea, I'll be working.''I wouldn't get in your way. We could just go for dinner... Or, I don't know, you could stay on for a few days? Maybe we could travel up to Mostar. See that famous bridge – I've been Googling Bosnia.' 'I have so many deadlines at the moment, I just don't think I'll be able to relax. Why don't we do something when I'm back? I'll plan something.'

'That's not the point.''What's not the point?''The point is, I'm supposed to plan something for you.''I really have to go now... let's talk when I'm back.''Sarah!' he blurted, warningly. She flinched.

'Yes?'

'Have you seen *Spiral*?''*Spiral*?''You'd love it. It's a French procedural... Sounds boring, but it's entirely binge-worthy.'

'I'll check it out when I get home.''No need to wait. I put the first three seasons on your laptop.''Right.''Does that feel intrusive?''No. Just weird.''I figured... I don't know. In case you needed distraction.''That's sweet of you. I have to run, though. Goodnight Jeremy. Night!'Her laptop was slung across her shoulder. She should change the password. Jeremy was frequently prescribing TV shows. Or movies. Or radio programmes. She could tell how worried he was by the number of titles recommended. Jeremy didn't like the thought of her being undistracted. He said it felt like sending her out into the cold.

The bus driver grew indecisive. He withdrew from the bus, leaned against it and made a phone call. Some of the passengers stared at him confusedly from the windows while others lit cigarettes outside. An old man offered Sarah a biscuit. She shook no. He offered again. She took it and put it in her pocket – which seemed to satisfy him – then fished out her pack of Camels.

The tobacco hissed, and her pulse quickened. Smoke rushed straight to the sensitive space in the back of her lungs, hitting the tender patch. She felt infused, every aching cell was fed. She dissolved. Nothing quite compared to that hit. When we discover a pleasure that is poisonous, Sarah reflected, we deform ourselves slightly. We taint.

Jeremy found it easy to live well. Easy to exercise, eat healthily and sleep sufficiently. He was built like a Ken doll and seemed to achieve this without much effort or sacrifice. She never smelled tobacco on his breath, or booze, or anything. His mouth tasted like distilled water.

'I'm here,' he'd said the last time they'd been together. They were in his bed and she'd been acting strange all night – flitting about the apartment, always finding reason to leave the room. Such nights were becoming more common. A restlessness that bordered on panic.

Jeremy did not understand such moods, but he noticed them.

'I'm here,' he kept saying when he got her to bed. He rubbed her back and drew her under the covers into a strange, tropical humidity. She inhaled a sweet vapour comprised of their body heat, their breaths, the oils evaporating from their skin. As he kneaded her muscles, she realised she was struggling to breathe; she worried there was not enough oxygen for both, that they were just recycling spent breaths between them. He pressed his damp nose against hers, became two huge eyes watching. She could see he was afraid, that he needed something; in his own way, Jeremy was also choking. Sarah focused on returning his caresses, on mimicking the signs of comfort, disguising the signs of asphyxiation. She can't have performed well. He was recommending TV shows, worried.

She dashed the cigarette after five drags, just shy of a satisfying hit.

The bus driver said something incomprehensible. He said it again and she realised he was speaking her name. It was time to go.

Sarah was happy to start moving and put a greater distance between herself and London. The night was pitch black; nothing could be seen from the windows apart from cats' eyes studding the highway. The lights stretched out, a static yellow line; for every two that were swallowed underfoot, another two appeared. This gave Sarah a feeling of suspension, of floating weightlessly in the dark.

It was originally opened in 2009 and called 'The War Hostel'. The next year, it was renamed 'The Atrocity Hostel' and finally, in 2014, perhaps in a bid for greater prestige, the 's' was dropped and it was renamed again, 'The Atrocity Hotel'. Sarah had stumbled across it in an article on the *New York Times* blog. Since then, she'd kept her eye on the place, reading its reviews on HostelBookers.com and the occasional write-ups on amateur travel blogs. She'd been fascinated by the tenor of these reviews, the writers proselytised, almost sombre in their praise. She sensed a story.

A week before her birthday, she felt a compulsion finally to write the piece. She had no idea what the angle would be. Her pitch, during the editorial meeting, was vague.

'Something to do with historical trauma,' she had said. The section editors looked at each other. 'Or maybe human nature,' she added. Michael, the editor-in-chief, leaned back in his chair.

'Good to know you're not getting bogged down in specifics,' he announced. 'Maybe you could follow it with a piece on language. Or time.' She shrugged and waited for him to commission the story. Which he did. The fact was, Sarah's last two pieces had gone viral, earning her a degree of creative freedom. Beyond that, she had clippings in *The Times*, *The Guardian* and *The Economist*. She was a seasoned writer, and the young site was paying for her credentials as much as her content.

The hostel was located in Alifakovak, a mostly residential neighbourhood in a hilly periphery of the city. The street sinewed wildly and Sarah trudged uphill in the thirty degree heat.

Glancing at her phone, she noticed three missed calls from Jeremy. She felt a pluck of guilt but steeled herself. Her birthday wish was to be left alone, to enjoy the pursuit.

All around, white houses glowed iridescent in the glare, making them painful to look at. Finally, she came upon a gravel path tucked between two homes, it led to a clearing of brittle yellow grass. In the centre stood the hotel, a great concrete slab of a thing, three storeys high.

She approached the door and rang. For a long time, nothing happened. She rang again.

After several minutes, the door swung open and he appeared. There were no lights within and he lingered briefly in the gloom before stepping out to meet her. The man was in full military garb: camo cargo trousers, an olive shirt and a thick bulletproof vest. He wore black leather boots and a helmet. His naturally dark skin was oddly sallow, bloodless and he stood silently, allowing her to take in the full sight of him, before speaking.

'Welcome to The Atrocity Hotel. You are Sarah?'

As the man squinted at her, adjusting to the brightness, Sarah did something that she had never done before. Usually, when she met subjects, she was a *tabula rasa*, unreadable, blank. Yet the instinct worked like a reflex, circumventing thought or self-censor. She tittered. Nervous laughter, the type that occurs when a very beautiful or very powerful person strikes you with an unexpected glance. It was odd; the man was possibly half her age, sweating profusely in his ridiculous costume. But he had a presence, an intensity.

'Yes, I'm Sarah,' her voice was level again.

'Adnan,' he said, holding out his hand. They shook and his fingers clamped hard on hers. They stood for a minute as if their meeting had reached a natural conclusion.

'I booked a two-night stay...' she said. She scratched the back of her calf with her foot then planted her feet firmly on the ground.

'I know,' he said.

He waited. She shrugged and smiled.

'You're a little early,' he said.

'The email said check-in is at one.'

'Wrong. Check-in is at two.' 'I can come back...' 'Your bed is ready so it makes no difference. But I wanted you to know: check-in is at two.'

He stepped aside. Within, the air was noticeably cooler. It smelled musty, old, like a thrift shop on a rainy day. The ground seemed to rock underfoot, making her first few steps unsteady. She noticed the walls tilted slightly inwards, like they were advancing, which created an illusion of movement and instability. Her body contracted slightly, as if to accommodate them.

Niamh Gordon grew up in Manchester and has a degree in English Language & Literature from Oxford. She writes short fiction, and is currently working on her first novel, *A Strange Cold Sun,* which investigates what happens when the boundary between memory and fiction blurs.

Millennial Pink
Extract from a story

PART 1

It is the end of a hot summer, and you have taken a new lover. He is gentle, watchful and calm. When he kisses you he cups your cheek with his palm. In the morning, after you have felt your way into consciousness, tracing the incumbent day along an inner thigh, a clavicle, shaping the world through touch, he rises from the bed you've been sharing and pads quietly downstairs to return with steaming fresh coffee in a percolator. He balances the coffee pot and two mugs in one hand, and two croissants on a plate in the other, and sets it all down unsteadily on the mattress. Usually you would not eat food in bed, but for him you make an exception. You drink the coffee black, bitter and bright, and tear the buttery pastry with your fingers, sucking the grease from each other's lips, flakes falling beneath the sheets.

You spend whole weekends in bed like this, marvelling at the intimacy of a new body beneath your fingertips. You place kisses on every inch of him, and he returns the favour, working steadily. You make love inquisitively, desirously. Your waking lives remain separate. Your universe is this bed, these languorous days and nights.

You are tall, wide-hipped and fair. You look as though you come from farming stock; thick-thighed and broad-shouldered, your hair like long straight hay. It falls heavy on your shoulders, and you sleep with it in one loose braid down your back. He tells you he has never made love to a body like yours, his equal in height and weight.

– My last girlfriend was tiny. Petite, I mean.

You imagine his thick hands on her aquiline frame, she all cheekbones and spine. He traces the fine hairs that lead from your belly button over the swell of your stomach down to your pelvis. He climbs over you, moves himself so that he is nestled between your legs, his chin resting lightly on your pubic bone. From your perspective he seems far away, in the valley beyond the mountain range of your breasts and belly. Breathing out, he teases you but, as your nipples harden, for a moment you think about his last lover. A small girl.

Fragile perhaps, like a bird.

Most days you work behind the reception desk in the air-conditioned foyer of a large office building. You take messages and connect calls, and hand out visitor stickers to unfamiliar faces, and smile blandly at other unfamiliar faces as they brandish their lanyards knowingly. There are at least fourteen separate businesses based in this building, and you know nothing about any of them.

It's a boring role, and you wile away the hours sharing cups of tea with Leonard, the security guard, and scrolling through social media feeds on your phone. You spend most of the time on Instagram, and about this Leonard is somewhat sceptical. He peers over your shoulder as you swipe through the profile of a singer whose music you don't particularly like but who posts pictures of her Labradoodle puppy in various carefully constructed situations. The puppy is cute; it's even cuter when posed wearing a pair of designer sunglasses and with its paw on the wheel of a convertible Mustang, as if it were cruising down Route 66 alone (caption: Paw-n to be wild!!!!).

You show Leonard. He looks at your phone screen, and then at you.

– That dog is very spoilt. It shouldn't be driving.

– Funny though, right?

– Not really.

Sometimes you read out thought-provoking quotes from a feminist meme account, or you'll show Len a piece of art posted by the Tate Modern page and then the two of you will enter into a disjointed discussion about art that you like and if you know why you like it and if that matters. Len is partial to David Hockney, but not the recent stuff with the iPad, which he says he finds distant and difficult to emotionally engage with. You say you think it's a fascinating move, which incorporates modern technology into an established creative practice, raising questions about the nature of producing an individual piece of art versus creating something that can be widely distributed in the exact same form as the original. Does each iteration of an iPad artwork count as something new, or are they all representations of one idea? Are they all imbued with the same creative drive and artistic merit contained within the flourish and whimsical sweeps of the original? Is there an original if it's digital? Len mumbles something about Andy Warhol and replication and you both feel out of your depth.

You are aesthetically cautious about the photos you post on your own profile. Your feed is filled with shadows; you are fascinated by the chiaroscuro you see in your world. You take iPhone pictures of empty coffee cups, an upturned cheek struck by sunlight, your bookshelf at dusk, and using a basic photo editing app you turn up the contrast and over-expose. One time Len asks you to post a picture of him. He thinks there is something profound to be captured within the purgatorial nature of working in a reception, and he poses in front of the revolving doors during an especially quiet afternoon. The sun streams through and offsets his silhouette.

In this fragmented way, your online interests bleed through into the workplace. These moments are the small highlights of your days.

Over the last weekend of August the heat is relentless and pushes on through the night. You sleep fitfully, and wake panicked and disorientated in the early hours. Your lover strokes your back, tries to soothe you. He is fair like you. His blond hair looks grey in the dim dawn light.

– Tell me about your favourite view, you say to him. Tell me what you see when you close your eyes.

He speaks to you of Cornish coasts, salt-bitten and wind-whipped, the sands silty and the taste of the sea heavy in the air, the roar of the swell and the empty, open Atlantic. Or maybe cascading Tuscan hills with a greener, brighter heat than you've ever experienced in England, fig trees drooping with fruit, thickly torn pieces of mozzarella piled onto a crimson sliced tomato drizzled in fragrant olive oil and eaten with fresh focaccia. Or maybe he tells you about the dawn-time hike he made up the steep side of the vast, strangely serrated mountain range near Barcelona, where from the highest point, Saint Jeroni, he watched the sun explode in the sky and burn reds, pinks, oranges, and he turned and took in the scale of the landscape, stretched miles out all the way to the sea, this the crest of Catalonia and deeply holy, and he waited on the top of the mountain, hoping that maybe, since he was so high up, it might be easy for God to reach down and speak to him, to show him some truth. But God did not, of course.

– Here, he says. I've got a photo of the monastery, it's not the best picture but it'll give a sense of the view. There's a funicular railway, which takes you up the side of the mountain, and we made our pilgrimage from there.

He reaches over you to take his phone from the bedside table and opens Instagram, scrolls through his own profile. Shuttered glimpses of the last year of his life flash by: drinks and friends and skies and art and his own face here and there, and then he stops at the image taken from the top of the funicular railway, but you barely see it, you're not really concentrating. Because the picture just before that is one of him with a dark-haired attractive girl, and you know that must be her. You only see it for a split second, but in it he has his arm around her waist and she is leaning her head against his chest like you are doing now. She looks thin.

Once the morning arrives properly he decides to go for an early run before the day gets too hot. You lie in bed on your phone, scrolling through an article about a government bailout of a failing bank while he laces his trainers. You read bits to him, little snippets as he limbers up, stretching quadriceps, hamstrings, deltoids.

I'm only doing five miles so I won't be long, he says.

He leans over and kisses the top of your head fondly. It is early. He smells of sleep.

You finish the article and hear the door slam downstairs. He will be out for maybe forty-five minutes, an hour tops, if he warms down slowly.

Absent-mindedly you pull up Instagram. He posted a photo of you together yesterday, and knowing that the image of you as a couple now exists online – that you have been officially incorporated into his feed as a part of his public life – makes your heart feel full. He takes nice photos: of his friends sharing a meal, or the dog at his family home. His parents, siblings, cousins, all smiling widely, their arms around one another, their same noses wrinkled in the same happy way, their love for each other worn clearly on their same family faces.

The app loads and you search his name and find the photo of the two of you. It's been relatively well received. A few likes, enough to reassure you that his online community are receptive to your presence. You tap onto the explore page and begin to scroll, consuming the photographs posted by accounts the app thinks you might be interested in based on who you already follow. You observe these posts without much thought, until there, bottom left, sharp-cheeked and smiling prettily, is her. The bird girl.

You tap the picture and it fills the screen. You stare at her face. In the photograph she sits in the garden of a wine bar that you think might be near your office block. Her waved dark hair just touches her bare shoulders. She wears a pale green sundress. She is laughing, red-lipped and blue-eyed. In one hand she holds a champagne glass, in the other a slim Vogue cigarette. Your heart is beating faster than before. She is flat-chested and angular, like you imagined.

Your finger hovers for a second, a cursory moment to let you pretend to yourself that there's a chance you might not do this, and then you tap on her name. Her profile doesn't load straight away; a small spinning disk rotates in the centre of the screen, indicating some unfathomable digital machinations occurring in the ether that will allow you to view into her life, its curated contents contained behind the glass. And then it's there, suddenly. Her whole feed. Open. You tap the photo of her in the sundress with the cigarette, staring out at you provocatively, the twist of her red lips, the wisp of smoke curling away off the top left of the photograph into the London air and you definitely do recognise the wine bar now, from other Instagram photos exactly like this – it's become a well-known spot precisely because of its eminently photographable ivy-draped walls and verdant leafy walkways, wall-climbing flowers dripping from pergolas and crowding the screen.

You can see the shadow of her sternum on her chest. The fingers holding the glass of expensive champagne are tipped by an expensive manicure. You think you actually recognise the dress from an advert for an expensive online retailer. There's a moment where you understand that your next action will cause you pain and then you choose it anyway. You put the tip of your finger to the screen, and you begin to scroll.

Francis Gosper is the recipient of the UEA Booker Prize Foundation Scholarship 2017/18. He studied at Columbia University. His novel *Little Boy* is a bildungsroman about the creation of the atomic bomb.

Little Boy
Extract from a novel

CHAPTER 7

The train having reached the port of Lobito, famous for its long spit, the boy was transferred, without being removed from his drum, onto a ship, and put to sea. It did not take him long to comprehend that his method of travel had changed, and that sea travel did not agree with him as rail travel had. Its motion was not rhythmic and calming like the motion of a train, but irregular and, according to his logic, terribly unnatural. Few children could resist the temptation to vomit under such circumstances. But vomiting was a luxury from which the boy was precluded, by his paralysis.

Much of the unpleasantness had to do with the nature of the hold, in which the corporation had felt it reasonable to quarter him. It was loud and dark and windowless. Its floorboards reeked with an offensive odor, the mingled outpourings very probably of esophaguses. The drums had been stacked on their sides and chained together so as not to roll about, with the drum containing his head and torso on the bottom. So he lay for the entirety of his marine journey in an unfortunate position, with the rust-holes pressing against his cheek, creating a nasty pain in the tumors, and the floorboards an inch from the pupil of his left eye.

Contortions and discomforts of this kind were not new to him of course, and did not account fully for his new dismay. More than anything it was sound that now tormented the boy, the sounds of the sea crashing ceaselessly against the walls, the creaking of the ship as though it was about to cave in, the roaring of its motor, the furious winds, the jostling of the body parts in the drums, the scrape of chains, the innumerable small sounds that conspired to inform him, tauntingly, that the ship was high on the wild sea, and all its cargo was dancing.

Though he did not articulate it in so many words to himself, the source of the boy's fear of the sounds of the hold was their resemblance to certain sounds he remembered from the mine. During those days, he had always been terrified of storms. It was the sense that everything was possessed, that the air and sky had turned hostile for reasons they refused to specify. When the storms became unbearable at the mine he had developed the habit of committing himself passionately to the strength and solidity of his shed, and taken solace in the fact that he had seen it withstand storms before. But here in the midst of the sea, in the midst of its sounds, which were to him a manifestation of the same vast petulance, the thought of his shed, which was far away, gave him no consolation.

Another inconvenience of this leg of the boy's journey was the lack of any device by which to distinguish day from night, or one day from the next. At that time, it was commonly known that for a cargo ship steaming at fifteen knots, a trip across the Atlantic took around one month. But the boy, having had no cause in his meager life to acquire this information, lay in his drum in ignorance, wondering, would it end soon, or would it go on? For when the eye is veiled there is no difference between the day's tumult and the night's tumult, or the day's calm and the night's calm. He could have counted the seconds, he who so loved to count, but even he did not have the patience for this, and his periods of sleep would have thrown this system into disarray. For how could he have determined if his sleeps were sleeps of ten hours or of ten minutes, sleeping and waking, as he did, in immaculate blackness? After a time he even began to confuse those moments when the storm lessened with those moments when his mind slipped into sleep, and the raging of the sea outside was replaced by a different raging within. And equally upon waking, he often could not be sure if a change was occurring in the weather, or in his consciousness. He told himself with certainty that he had pined through many weeks in the belowdecks, but moments – or perhaps days – later, he told himself with the same certainty that he had endured only a night or two.

For a while he thought about escaping. But he soon realised, upon consideration of his paralysis, his sealed drum, the chains, and the storm on every side, the futility of this notion, and resolved that he would face his predicament for as long as it continued. He told himself, in a tone of great severity, as he had done a few times at the mine, that to be afraid was no longer of any use. If something was not of any use it made no sense to do it, of this he was confident. Whoever had sent him away, he reasoned, had deemed him old enough to travel by himself. He put his faith therefore in his keepers, as he had always done, calling upon that same ardent irrational sense that they knew what was best for him.

In the pretty future the boy had long imagined, in which he flung his body about on its feet all day and night in the joy of movement, unbothered by storms, and spent his time among crowds of friends, this incident would comprise one of the tales with which he regaled them, and they would laugh and congratulate him on his pertinacity. Here he drew upon his reserves of hope and delusion, which were great, in spite of his unfortunate acquaintance with reality. Few infantile minds could have dredged such practicable nonsense as the boy's. He was similar in this respect to his advocate Dr Szilard. Thus he began, with prolonged efforts, to gird himself against the years and decades of displeasure he foresaw in the ship.

Little did he know, as he resolved himself to these conclusions, that day by day his ship was gaining on its destination. And the captain, high above the boy, in a tiny box of his own, was soon congratulating himself on having made good time, and for not having disappointed the corporation, whose representatives had ordered him to make haste, and was chafing to inflict himself on the nearest woman he could afford. And on the horizon ahead, narrow and trembling, a sliver of grey was emerging, like an utterance of the sea, and gradually increasing in size.

Finally he arrived. It was November, 1941. A handsome harbor appeared, unseen by the boy. It was a scene that his doctors had gazed on five or ten years earlier – Dr Teller, Dr Bethe, Dr Szilard, Dr Fermi, and so many other illustrious members of the medical profession. For a moment, as the steamer drew within sight of the large, strange-complexioned woman on the shore, it seemed that the boy was going to follow them, succumb also to the pull of those waters which had sucked so many scattered human lives into one place. But the ship swung west and, turning off a long way south of Ellis Island, made its way towards the Bayonne Bridge. Down in the hold, the boy barely registered a change in the sounds and motions of the ship. Curled naked, wearied by a month's darkness, his head buried down under his stiff shoulders, and the flitters of his rump uppermost in the dark of the drum, and swaying back and forth, up and down, he tried to think of anything but the present moment. He knew nothing of the buildings or the bridges, nothing of the overpeopled streets, and hadn't the faintest idea that cities even existed.

But then a curious thing happened, which was to alter his understanding. It was at the last moment. The ship had been moored for a while by the quay. As a little group of silent men were rolling the drums up on deck, the boy's eye happened to align for a second with one of the rust-holes, and through it he caught a glimpse, one glimpse, across the water masked with mist, of the city. It was all pale blue. For a second he gazed with his little eye on its spires and towers. Then every thought he had hitherto had on his journey, and every thought he had hitherto had, so it seemed, in his life, rose up off him like the smoke around a struck match and, like the smoke, dissipated. There are few things that man has made which correspond to the span and shape, the beauty and the ugliness, of what is called the soul – New York City is one of them. The boy recognised it at once as something he had known all his life. He could not explain this feeling. He felt he was looking at something that could not possibly exist, and yet he could trace, with his own eyes, the physical space stretching between him and it. Pale and enormous it stood, shimmering in the mild morning. As he rolled on in the dark of the drum, bouncing and bumping on his old wounds and growths, along the deck and down onto the wharf, he could think of nothing but the city and the vague beckoning look it had given him.

Jenny Hedger is a Mexican-American writer from Tucson, Arizona and winner of the Tucson Writers' Studio 2015 Write-to-Read Contest. Formerly a social worker and now a part-time barista, her writing explores themes of family, mental illness, and poverty in the Sonoran Desert. She lives with her boyfriend and two cats in Norwich, England.

Head Above Water
The opening of a novel

POTENTIAL

'If we all did the things we are capable of, we would astound ourselves.'

According to the poster above Ms Montgomery's desk, the guy who invented the lightbulb said that. Which is easy for him to say. He invented the lightbulb. If I invented the lightbulb, I'd probably say that kind of cheesy shit, too.

Since I showed up to school with a black eye two weeks ago, I've spent a lot of time in this office looking at these stupid motivational posters about potential and hard work and success and overcoming hardship. At least they cover up the ugly gray paint the district uses in all of the offices and classrooms here.

I want to tear down the one about not letting other people determine your attitude, and wrap it around Mr Jones across the hall like a blanket. He always looks like he's about to have a nervous breakdown whenever a kid leaves his office. Mr Jones is in charge of discipline and so he deals with the kids who get caught having sex in the library or mouth off to the teachers or get into fights. He's got his master's in psychology or something. I can see the degrees on the wall behind him in his office from here. I don't really hang out with those kids but it doesn't take some expensive piece of paper to know that most of them have it bad at home and other kids are just idiots or don't care. I'm not that smart, but at least I'm not an idiot. Sometimes when I get caught ditching, they send me to Mr Jones and he runs his hands through his hair and asks if I'll sign an attendance contract and agree to show up for the next couple of weeks and sometimes I say yes just because I feel bad for him.

And I don't have it *that* bad at home. My stepmom, Brandi, caught me on the side of my face the other morning with a coffee cup, but she was drunk and not actually aiming for me. She felt pretty guilty and that put her in a crappy mood the rest of the day. Then Ms Montgomery called Child Protective Services and now I'm stuck meeting with the school counselor every couple of days to make sure I'm OK until CPS decides what to do about me. They told me if I don't come to school on a regular basis, CPS will show up at my house. I'd drop out but then I'll probably have to get a job and I'm not all that excited to start bagging groceries at Mortenson's, where Brandi works. Brandi's always nagging me about 'contributing to the household' and promises to get me a weekend job there, but then I'd have to spend even more time than I already do with her and she's just as annoying sober as she is drunk.

'Ellie? Are you OK?'

'Huh? Oh, yeah, I'm fine.'

Ms Montgomery twirls her crunchy, curly brown hair around her left pointer finger and raises her too-thin eyebrows at me. 'I was asking how things are going at home. Are you and your stepmother still... having conflict?'

Ms Montgomery's all right. She's been telling me since freshman year to put more effort into school, even though things 'might be rough at home', because she 'cares' about me and talks about my 'potential.' I tell her that she might as well just give up on me because I'm failing and about to drop out and why does everyone act like they care so much? When I do that, she shoves a book or a magazine at me. Something to shut me up, but that's OK because then I'm not expected to talk. Today she's just checking in.

'Everything's fine,' I tell her for about the millionth time. I know that kids whose parents beat them up probably say that all the time, but for once I'm telling the truth. Brandi's pretty selfish and she's definitely not very smart, but she doesn't hit me.

'You know you can always tell us if you need anything, right?'

'Yeah.'

'I know you probably don't trust us much anymore after the CPS call, but we're all here for you. We all want you to succeed and if there's any way we can help out, we will.'

'I know.'

Ms Montgomery sighs and smiles at me with her lips pressed together. She does that a lot during our meetings.

After she gives up on the heart-to-heart, she grabs another book from one of the big bookshelves behind her desk and hands it to me. This office is tiny, but she's made it home-y. Most of the gray space around the motivational posters is covered with graduation pictures of old students and kids' artwork and she's crammed a couple of comfy, cushioned green chairs across from her desk.

I flip through the book (*Ophelia Speaks* this time) while Ms Montgomery fills out a little blue hall pass so I can go back to Health. At first it looks like a poetry book, but some of the pages look more like regular stories. I stuff it in my bag and leave. Ms Montgomery's nice, but she doesn't get it.

My Health teacher, Mr Rubin, does. He knows I'm just killing time here. He doesn't bother me, except to look at me like I'm a loser. There aren't any motivational posters in his classroom, just ugly, old-style gray metal chaired desks, a few diagrams of the human body and posters that say things like, 'AIDS: ARE YOU AS SAFE AS YOU THINK YOU ARE?' Rubin's the kind of guy who'd make up the seating chart according to how smart he thinks we all are if he thought he could get away with it.

I leave the office and flash my hall pass at the monitors, who just nod. They try to look way too serious in their neon-orange vests, jean shorts, and mirrored sunglasses, patrolling the halls for ditchers and fights like wannabe mall cops.

Mr Rubin's classroom is in the gym basement and I walk the long way between the buildings, instead of cutting across the sports fields, hoping some people are behind the gym smoking so I don't have to go back in right away. No one's hanging out back there. It's almost noon and there's no shade and nowhere to sit. It's too expensive to grow grass, so apart from the football and baseball and soccer fields, everything is red rock and cactus all over. The spiked, wrought-iron fence that runs around the entire campus is painted the same beige as the buildings. I would say it looks like a prison, but the spikes on the fence curve up and out toward the street and the landscaping is probably a little better.

I hate Rubin's classroom. Aside from the crappy posters that are supposed to scare us, it's always cold and damp down here so I always have to bring a sweater to school, no matter how hot it is outside or if the heating is on everywhere else. Then, there's Mr Rubin himself; he's probably cold and damp on the inside too. When I slide into the desk closest to the door, he's talking about some car accident he was in as a teenager and how he got rocks stuck in his scalp and that's why we should all wear seatbelts. He's short and squat and bald with a long goatee and he gives me the creeps. He talks for a while more about some other stuff I don't pay attention to, then assigns us some bookwork from the 'Making Healthy Choices' chapter. There are some dumb multiple-choice questions ('_____ causes lung cancer. Is it a) marijuana b) smoking c) French kissing or d) not wearing a seatbelt?') and a section that asks me to write about a time I felt 'peer pressure' and how did I respond? I write a few sentences about saying no to drugs, put my paper in the assignment basket on the table next to the door, and spend the rest of class peeling my chipped, glittery nail polish.

When the bell rings, I jump up and I'm almost out the door before I hear him call me back.

'Ellie, I need to see you before you go.'

I hate the way he says my name, like he's flicking at it with his tongue.

I sit on top of a desk in the front row. He's not even looking at me when he talks.

'You keep missing my class. You're going to fail by default.'

I shrug. 'I'm pretty sure I have a D in this class. And I have to meet with Ms Montgomery. I don't get to choose which class they pull me out of.' I'm just lucky that way.

I dig the crumpled hall pass out of my pocket and hand it to him. He sets it down on his desk without looking at it.

'Yeah. Well, I'll be having a chat with Ms Montgomery about the impact of these meetings on your grade in my class. Health isn't being offered during summer school and you need to pass to graduate on time.'

'OK,' I say. I don't know what I'm supposed to do now.

Rubin leans back in his chair and combs his beard with his stubby little fingers. 'Go, then,' he says, impatiently. 'You'll be late for your next class.'

There's that loser look again.

Faye Holder is working on her first novel *Bugger Bognor*. It is a satirical take on what happens to a young woman after completing a journey of social mobility. Despite her improved career prospects, Faith finds herself caught between two social groups, never quite feeling at home in either.

Bugger Bognor
Extract from a novel

CHAPTER 1

I dump my heavy case in the hallway and step into the newly fitted kitchen: white, shiny, handleless cabinets line the walls. A sudden pfff sound takes half a year off my life. 'Fuck me,' I say, having nearly lobbed the milk across the kitchen. I'd forgotten Mum's a big fan of motion sensor air fresheners. They're everywhere. Navigating my parents' home is like running a gauntlet of poisonous sprinklers in a hothouse. At any moment you run the risk of losing an eyeball to an air freshener disguised as a pebble. It would be an ignominious end, I'd rather be flattened by their new American-style fridge.

The monolithic black fridge sits at the far end of the kitchen, just before the dining room. It's my parents' new favourite purchase, and I have to admit it is an impressive beast of a machine, if also a slightly extravagant buy for a retired couple in their sixties. 'We keep everything in it now,' Mum had said, excitedly over the phone. 'All the sauces *and* the jams.' 'Brilliant,' I'd said, while pushing my limp salad around the plate. 'Your dad loves the icemaker. You know how he likes a whisky every night. That's what swung it really. He was tired of filling up those little plastic bags.' I grip the handle and swing the door open. There's a pleasant weight to it. It feels substantial and well-made, like a luxury car. I peer inside, but the fridge looks like any other. I slot the milk Mum asked me to pick up into an empty space and let the door close with a satisfying thump. I'm not thirsty, but I can't resist trying out the legendary icemaker. The ice rumbles down the chute and clatters into the tall glass with a satisfying ping, ping, ping. 'Damn,' I say, to Ed the ginger cat who's ambling across the kitchen towards me, 'that is good.'

On the granite counter top there's a note: *Faith, could you water your dad's tomatoes if you're not busy. Thanks. Mum. X*

Ed looks up at me and meows. He wants feeding.

You're never a guest in your parents' house.

'Fucking witch,' says Dad, at the TV before shoving another fork of lettuce into his mouth, while at dinner that evening.

Mum sighs, as I try to suppress a smile.

It's always a surprise to hear Dad swear, but politicians, especially Conservative ones, bring out his spikier side.

A large flat-screen TV, a hand-me-down from the living room, hangs massively on the wall in the corner of the dining room at the far end of the knocked-through kitchen. There's a documentary on about the Brighton bombing at the Grand Hotel in 1984.

Thatcher emerges from a police station, surrounded by worried looking men in suits. A reporter whose grey hair matches his coat throws out his arm.

'Life must go on as usual,' she says, into his outstretched microphone.

She's hurried into the back of a black Jag, which zooms out of shot, leaving a trail of journalists in its wake.

'Me and your dad had just started going out when that happened, hadn't we, love?'

'Mmm-huh,' says Dad, through a mouthful of food.

It's a mistake watching this documentary. It's bound to lead to an argument, but turning off the TV isn't an option, because then we'd have to talk to each other.

'They came close, didn't they?' says Mum.

I know what Dad's going to say before he even opens his mouth. I can see him revving up to it.

'Not close enough,' he says.

Bingo.

An older Thatcher is now being interviewed in a cosy sitting room, her hair as resolute as ever.

'She got the job done though, didn't she?' Mum says, predictably, sitting at the opposite end of the dinner table to Dad.

Here we go, back on the old rollercoaster. I shouldn't get involved. Just leave them to it.

'She never took any nonsense, especially not from Europe,' says Mum.

'Especially not from them miners either.' The words escape my lips before I can stop them.

'I didn't mean it like that,' she says, with a tired expression. 'Besides, you can talk.'

'Pardon?' I say, a piece of cucumber hovering between my mouth and the plate.

'Private banking's hardly blue-collar, is it?'

'It was a stopgap,' I say.

'Big gap,' Mum says, raising her eyebrows. 'Nine years.'

I don't react, because I know she's right. I've become the monster I used to rage against.

'If it wasn't for her, me and your dad would never have this house.'

What I want to say is, *I wish the IRA had bloody killed her,* but what I actually say is 'hmm.'

Mum smiles. She knows I'm beat.

CHAPTER 2

The next morning I'm woken by a pigeon cooing. Cooing is not the right word. Cooing is pleasant. This pigeon sounds like he has a chest infection. He wheezes in and out. I leave him be for a time, thinking he'll get bored and fly off, but he doesn't. After five minutes of asthmatic pigeon wheezing, I can't take it anymore. I lift my head from the pillow and poke it out of the open window. The pigeon is perched on the aerial fixed to the gable wall above my window. I'm not a violent person, but if I had a rifle, I'd have the perfect shot. I don't have a gun, so instead I clap my hands and shout, 'bugger off!' The pigeon doesn't move, doesn't even flinch, though he does stop wheezing.

I flop my head back onto the pillow and stare up at the dusty light fitting in the centre of the room. I think about Jon waking up in the flat his parents are helping us buy in London. I should text him. The pigeon begins cooing again. 'Fucker.' I look around the room for something to use as a makeshift poking device, maybe I can push him off his perch, but then it occurs to me that I'm the one invading his personal space, so I leave him be, and I get up.

My old bedroom is full of remnants from my childhood: postcards of painted nudes, a stuffed teddy bear holding a big red heart, and a bookshelf full of well-thumbed classics. There are other items now too, ones I don't recognise because they aren't mine. They're a spill over from the rest of the house: piles of folded clothes on an ironing board, an old computer, and boxes of Christmas decorations.

When I reach the kitchen, a note is waiting for me on the counter:
Faith, if you're not busy could you pay my cheque in? See you later.
Dad. X
I sigh and flick the kettle on.

A few hours later, I walk along the promenade to town, foregoing the quicker path through the council estate.

On the pier, despite warning signs promising fines and/or death, a group of young lads take their chances jumping off into the sea. They slam into the water twenty-odd feet below with a big foamy splash. I wish I had their courage until one mistimes his entry and surfaces winded. On the beach below, two young fathers trudge carefully across mounds of unstable shingle, ferrying ice creams and bottles of coke to their sweltering families who sit on brightly-coloured deckchairs, their skin turning pink. I always forget that people actually come on holiday to Bognor.

The bank is lovely and cool. A beautiful breeze drifts down from the air-conditioning vent above and across my lily-white neck and shoulders. I stand in a queue populated with pensioners wearing pastel colours and sandals and complaining about the weather.

'I wouldn't mind but it's that oppressive heat,' says an old woman to her friend, as she fans her face with her pension book.

Opposite the queue, an elderly hunched-over man is struggling to work a self-service paying-in machine. I can't figure out if he's deaf or just annoyed. He's shouting at a smartly dressed lady who's trying to help him deposit his cheque.

'I don't like machines,' he says, loudly. 'I like to talk to people.'

The queue edges fractionally forward, and I feel a tap on my bare shoulder.

'Hello stranger,' says the voice behind me.

I turn and see a face that seven years ago was as familiar as my own.

'All right?' I stumble.

CHAPTER 3

Sadie pours a fourth teaspoon of sugar into a stripy mug of tea. She always did have a sweet tooth. 'When did you get back?'

The walls of the caff are lined with black and white photos of Bognor in its Victorian heyday. Sadie and I sit opposite one another at a table by the window. A freestanding fan by the counter moves hot air about the small room.

'Yesterday,' I say, wiping a bead of sweat from my nose, as I scan her face, taking in the details that used to be so familiar: the vibrant auburn hair and the cluster of freckles around her nose.

'Just visiting?' she says.

'Uh... yeah,' I say, the sentence petering out.

'Oh right.'

Sadie doesn't ask any follow-up questions. She would've done back in the day when we were best friends, but now she just stares into her tea.

Sadie asks, 'Still doing the banking?'

'Yeah,' I say, slowly nodding.

Sadie and I used to be able to talk about anything, but now I'm struggling for a conversation starter. I find myself blurting out, 'How's the factory?' As soon as the words leave my mouth, I realise my mistake. 'Oh shit! I'm sorry.'

Sadie smiles sadly and shrugs her shoulders. 'Two years in September.'

'Time flies,' I say, looking at the friend I've not seen in seven years.

'Yeah,' Sadie says, glancing up from her tea. 'It does.'

I can't hold her gaze. I look down at the salt shaker I've been passing through my fingers and ask, 'Do you still hear from anyone from Shoreline?'

'A few.'

Sadie stirs a teaspoon round and round her mug. We both stare at it. We're the only customers in the Rendezvous Café apart from a skinny old man at a table in the corner carefully spreading butter to all four corners of his toast.

'What happened to everyone?' I ask, too belatedly.

'Some retired: Deborah, Reg, Barb. Some of the younger girls went to Tesco. Tammy's at Sainsbury's. Pervy Dave's over in—'

'And what about you,' I say. 'What have you been up to?'

A look of uncertainty flickers across Sadie's face before she blinks it away and becomes suddenly engrossed in the scene outside the window. The traffic ebbs and flows with the red and green of the lights opposite the café.

'I've been doing... bits and bobs,' she says, her eyes following someone as they pass by the window.

'Oh, right.'

I too turn to look out of the window. We both stare off across the street, watching the lights as they flash from amber to red.

'I'm thinking of moving home,' I say, surprising myself.

'Really?' Sadie thinks for a second. 'Why?' comes her inevitable reply. 'You're doing so well.'

'I don't feel like I... belong there. I feel like I'm living someone else's life.'

I turn the salt shaker round on its bottom in the middle of the table. Sadie and I watch it rotate in the empty space between us.

Sadie opens her mouth to say something, but then closes it again.

'Maybe I should've stayed at the factory,' I say.

'Don't be bloody ridiculous,' says Sadie, throwing me one of her old tired looks. 'You'd have gone mad.'

I know she's right. I couldn't have stayed at the factory, but then I can't stay at the bank either.

Sarah Hopkinson was born in Gloucestershire in 1991. After graduating from Harvard University with a degree in English Literature, she worked for an academic think tank before training and working as an English teacher in London. She is working on a novel.

On My Insides
An extract from a novel

Leonora suffers from an incurable tapeworm and the fear of being touched. She has been admitted to the Willow – a hospital in East Anglia for women with similarly incurable and elusive illnesses. In this chapter, she leaves the Willow and goes for a walk with a fellow patient, Tiger, who is a mute. Prior to this, Leonora has discovered that she can touch Tiger without pain.

I met Tiger behind *Murmurati*. Marguerita had told me about a path that cut across the fens, clinging to a straight ditch. When I'd woken up this morning, the sky had been watery blue. Now it was the colour of vanilla ice cream, a stratus cloud stretched across it. The cloud cover only made it hotter, all that heat trapped in the narrow space between heaven and earth. I rounded the building and saw Tiger's strange form beneath a willow tree. A murmuration took off into the sky above her and it could have been a wallpaper pattern climbing towards the ceiling.

I pointed up at the sky and said 'Stratus,' not knowing what else to say. She looked up, exposing her long neck.

'The word comes from the Latin *strato*, literally meaning layer. Stratus clouds are different to others because they're so thin, no more than a fog bank,' I said, pausing, but her eyes were still glued to the sky. 'I'm not interested in clouds,' I continued. 'No more than anyone else. But I'm interested in their names. Cloud nomenclature is very literal. Cumulonimbus comes from the Latin *cumulus* meaning heap, and *nimbus* meaning rainstorm. If you were to look at a cross-section of a cumulonimbus, you couldn't describe it as anything but a heap of rain. Their names describe physical appearance and so there's no metaphorical implication there or room for confusion. It's the type of language which cuts like crystal on your tongue.'

I was looking at the sky so I didn't see her mouth swing open.

'And is that something you want?' she asked. 'To cut your tongue?'

Her voice didn't sound as I'd imagined. Instead, it had a kind of power. As though words were things that could be tamed.

'I'd rather a cut than something like honey which can glue your mouth shut,' I said.

'But both could have the same ends. Shutting you up, I mean,' she said.

'Maybe that's what we both want.'

She smiled and her face changed. There was suddenly a kind of lightness to it, despite the dark shadows under her eyes and the sunken cheeks.

Her speaking did not shock me. I'd known she would from the moment I'd seen her crouched below the trees.

We shimmied down a steep bank that led to the path. She had on a green raincoat that swirled around her legs and I imagined it was a cape. She'd gathered her long hair on top of her head in a ponytail and it swayed gently as she walked, threads of black dangling behind her ear. I wanted to curl one around my little finger and pull. As we walked, the back of her hand brushed mine. Cool and soft, like a marble counter top or the inside of a window pane in winter. Soon, we left the Willow behind and the open fens felt suddenly grander. They made me feel inconsequential, seeing my problems as transitory things, no more destructive than one brief gust of wind. Far below us – because the ditch had been dug so deeply – water the colour of an unfilled television channel flowed slowly. It smelt of decayed fish. Up ahead, a line of trees were the colour of Dijon mustard, confirming that the seasons had turned, or were turning, despite the suffocating heat. It was difficult to remember time as something which instigated actual change when, for over a year, it had only marked perpetual stasis. Sometimes I wanted to get worse if only to prove my body was still alive.

'How come you can speak to me?' I asked.

She stopped on the bank, becoming a single birch tree in the middle of a field.

'I'm not sure,' she said slowly. 'This is the first time I've spoken in almost two years.'

'How does it feel?'

'Strange. Inadequate. There are two years of thoughts that want to come out, but I don't know where to start.'

'Tell me about what you were doing before all of this,' I said.

We started walking again, tentatively, matching our movements to our speech. Our arms swung in closer, then moved apart again. Her raincoat brushed my elbow.

'I used to make urns,' she said. 'Funeral urns. I trained as a ceramicist but then everyone else started making trendy, rough-edged tableware. I'd look at my clay and all I could see was how it would get swept up into some cliché vision of earthy domesticity, only to be shattered by a sticky-fingered child and then forgotten about. Not that I wanted the things I made to be worshipped. But I wanted to feel their purpose was somehow more.'

'More what?'

'Substantial perhaps. Although that's probably not the right word either. I liked the idea, I suppose, that someone would inhabit what I'd made, as though it were a body, or a new body. One that wasn't subject to the exigencies of human time, but to longer time instead. But then I also liked the idea that funeral urns might serve a purpose other than holding ashes. So, it could be decorative as well as memorial, or a place to put things. I even made one which served as an umbrella stand in addition to containing someone's great-aunt.'

'Did people buy them?'

'The decorative ones. The multi-purpose ones were a harder sell so I stopped making those in the end.'

'What about making urns with different compartments,' I said, 'so, eventually, it might contain a whole family?'

She laughed. Her long fingers grazed my hand again. I felt a tingle and then a shock of electricity. The effect of a tactile encounter with something not of my matter. Once, in Scotland, Spike and I had come across a beach full of washed-up jellyfish. They'd looked like translucent sea shells, their ink-blue tentacles spilling over the sand. Later, we'd learnt they weren't jellyfish but Portuguese man o' wars, whose tentacles can grow to one hundred and sixty feet long. The Portuguese man o' war is not a single organism, but a colonial organism made up of specialised, individual animals. Although individual, these animals are fully integrated, which means they cannot survive on their own. Her touch was not like a jellyfish sting, but the re-attachment of two, disconnected polyps.

'I'll look into it if I ever get out. I'll make one to house the two of us,' she said, her gaze lingering over me like a tongue.

The grassy path turned into gravel. We continued until it came to a small yard filled with disused farming equipment. Orange tractor arms tumbled together like mannequin limbs. Long grass rippled around the rusted body of a harvester. Beside the hump of a car door, a large metal bucket overflowed with grey water. Metal wire grew from the ground like brambles. Old car tyres might have been disgorged from the earth itself, not left here to rot. Tiger picked her way through the detritus. She stepped so lightly she might have been an antelope. I stopped to inspect a spade protruding from the ground. Grass entwined it; more organic now than constructed. I followed her to a large wooden crate and sat beside her, our legs swinging towards the grass.

'How long do you think all of this has been here?' she asked.

'Maybe months, or even decades,' I said.

Sunlight caught her on the chin.

'It seems to symbolise something, don't you think?' I asked.

'What something?'

'Capitalism perhaps,' I said. 'That all we do is accumulate things, and then discard them. Shoring up all the waste in places where no one ever goes so we don't have to look at it. Kind of like the Willow. People lock us up so they don't have to think about the crazies like us.'

I felt a smattering of water droplets brush my lips. I licked. Moisture soothed the fissures. Tiger looked at me. The heat had squashed me into the ground, but Tiger pulled me straight again. I leant over and kissed her. I could not see her eyes because they were closed. But I knew they were the colour of rainclouds. I wanted this moment to wrap around everything else in my life. Warm breeze cut across the back of my neck. The wooden crate shifted beneath us and I wondered where the wood had come from. Below us, in the ground, earthworms moved through their desiccating caverns, hoping for rain.

She pulled away and smiled. Her hand braided mine as though we were part of the same body. She leapt up and grabbed something off the floor.

'Look at this,' she said, holding up a large clay pot curved like a woman's body. It had a handle on either side and was slick with red mud. Her eyes were wide. Time peeled back and she became a child again, giddy and uncontainable, and her slim body shrank into itself.

'If you could take anything from here, what would it be?' she asked, laughter sneaking from her mouth.

I laughed too, even though I didn't want to.

'This crate,' I said.

'Why?'

'It would be somewhere to hide inside.'

Wind blew the smile off her face. Behind her, the Willow's glass walls glinted in the distance. I had lost track of myself and strayed into terrain I no longer recognised.

'We should be heading back,' I said.

Tiger nodded, reasserting her solemn shape. She dropped the pot to the ground and it skidded across the earth, crashing into the harvester's ribcage, then picked her way back through the waste and headed towards the track. I paused and felt the sinking of substance into time. For a moment, I wanted to sink down with it.

I caught up with Tiger and pushed my little finger into her fist. Her hand opened, curling around mine. A scruffish smile lingered on her face.

'What happened?' I asked. 'What got you in here?'

She clenched my hand harder. Above us, the sky looked threateningly white.

'I wondered what would happen if I mixed ashes into the clay itself instead of putting the ashes inside the urn. It seemed a better way of preserving them. Ashes to ashes, dust to dust. Ash becoming clay. Some kind of cyclical rhythm to everything. I guess I wanted something more to come of a person than decay.

'Obviously, I didn't tell clients about this. I knew none of them would appreciate their relatives becoming ceramic. Instead, I'd replace the ashes with the contents of a vacuum cleaner. Except, somehow, one of the clients found out. I never worked out how. Perhaps she'd spent a long time examining her mother's remains and knew the difference between that and vacuum dust. She reported me to the police. Tried to get me arrested. Although, in the end, all they could really charge with me was vandalism of property which couldn't be held up in a court of law as she'd given me her mother's ashes willingly. In the end, the judge deemed me psychologically inept. So, I ended up here,' she said.

'When did you stop speaking?' I asked.

She smiled, but didn't answer.

Somehow I knew this was a question I shouldn't have asked. Sometimes, it seemed impossible to explain things, even to ourselves.

Our shadows arched ahead of us along the bank, like the future waiting for us to catch up.

Naomi Ishiguro was born in London in 1992. Before starting at UEA she worked as a bookseller and bibliotherapist at Mr B's Emporium of Reading Delights in Bath, and got a BA in English from University College London. She is currently working on a collection of linked short stories.

Compass Points

Extract from a short story

'How many times can anyone pack and repack the same suitcase without feeling amazed, just amazed, that they still haven't made a decision yet about what to do, where to go, or whether, indeed, it is truly necessary for them to go anywhere at all? Manhattan is not what I expected. It's darker, for one thing, being always in the shade of its own skyscrapers, and it's both more and less methodical, in ways that do not square with the ways in which I am and am not methodical – that is to say, I understand neither the exacting grid system of the streets, nor the human tumult that fills them. Yet here I am, neither fully committed to being here nor fully resolved to go, keeping this battered suitcase ready in our too-large wardrobe, just in case something comes to me when I least expect it – some dream, some magical solution to the problem of my life, which, as it stands, and as it has been standing for the past one hundred and twenty-six days now, will not fit together into any kind of resolution, as if each of those days is an individual piece from a separate jigsaw puzzle, and they're all jumbled together in a box, undecided as yet about the extent to which they'll ever be able to fit themselves together into a new, completed picture.

And then, of course, there's a question there – about the extent to which that actually matters. Maybe I'm content to be a muddle of jigsaw pieces, instead of a solved image? I mean, when I think about some of the sorts of things those puzzles depict... old English trains, old English train stations, Japanese mountains, Swiss mountains, zebras, parrots, mountain lions, lynxes, budgies, wild cats, kittens for old ladies to look at and compare with the memory of their own dear departed pets... when I think about those sorts of things, I am not sure I want to be like that at all. Perhaps it is preferable to be a little less cohesive, a little less clear.

On the days when my fiancé is out at work, which is most days, even some Saturdays – she's very driven – I remove the suitcase from the too-large wardrobe (I say 'too-large' because it takes up half our bedroom, and is just obviously bigger than the scale of the life any reasonable kind of person would lead) and I spend twenty minutes or so looking over the contents. Sometimes I remove an item, and sometimes I add something that hadn't occurred to me as being necessary before. This morning, for instance, I added a compass – because it's always useful, I've decided, to know where you are in relation to something fixed, even if you are unsure of where you're going.

Some mornings, I'll take every single item out of the suitcase, laying them all out in a line on the bedcovers, and I'll handle each object in turn, checking them over carefully – *envelope of dollars, envelope of sterling, full hip flask of London dry, keys to my apartment, keys to my parents' house all the way back in North Finchley, jar of pickles, lucky Smurf,* and now – *compass.* Then, when I've completed my rounds I'll replace the objects back in the case, click the catches shut, and consider whether that morning will be the morning I seize the suitcase by the handle and step out of the apartment with it, never to return again – at least not in this version of my life.

Perhaps in a parallel universe I'd set out into the streets of New York, knuckles getting whiter as I grip the peeling leather of the suitcase handle and walk all the way across the bridge to Williamsburg. How different that bridge is from Battersea Bridge, from Blackfriars Bridge – how different from any of those old bridges over the Thames! Williamsburg Bridge with its triumphal hugeness, its ostentatious suspension cables, and the full half hour of your time it demands once you've decided to commit to it. I'd probably consider walking even further on the other side, but stop in a café instead, for something to eat. So there I'd sit – at the counter, maybe, or alone, off to one side, at a small Formica table, with the still-unopened suitcase resting by my feet so that I can feel it brush reassuringly against my ankle every time I cross and recross my legs – while the working day clatters its way through the city surrounding me, and people in crisp shirts, sharp suits, smart shoes, or eschewing all of that in incongruously cool, smart-casual millennial-wear, move from morning coffee and post to emails to meetings to lunch to meetings to coffee to emails to just... standing for a moment by the office rubber plant and simply staring through the floor-to-ceiling glass windows, out at the street.

I might have left the café by this point – this parallel me in this parallel life in this parallel version of New York. I might even happen to be walking right down that very same Brooklyn street containing that very same fancy reconditioned factory hipster-chic media office in which at that exact moment that particular employee – the one standing by the rubber plant – happens to be staring out of the window. Our eyes might happen to meet. And although he looks nothing like me – nothing at all, really, we don't even have the same colour eyes, or the same colour hair – something about his expression would remind me of yet another alternative possibility of myself, and I'd realise I had to go back. So, without giving this accidentally significant office worker even a smile or a nod that might acknowledge our completely random moment of meaningful interaction through a window, I'd turn on my heel and walk all the way through the red-brick Brooklyn streets and over the bridge to Manhattan, all the way up the East Side and through the Park (Central Park as seen from the air – what a vast gap in the density of buildings! What an empty, vacant space to discover at the centre of everything!) not stopping until I was through the narrow blue door and up the three flights of stairs to our apartment, where I'd be home just in time to shut the suitcase away in the too-large wardrobe and to tidy my hair before I hear Rachel – that's my fiancé, by the way, her name is Rachel – before I hear Rachel's key turn in the lock.

'Hi honey,' she'd say. 'You been out?'

'Only to the grocery store,' I'd say, returning her kiss hello.

'You get anything for dinner?'

'No, only pickles again' – because most likely I would have picked up a few jars of pickles on the way back. I think I like jars of pickles so much because they seem to share in my condition of suspended stasis. I feel companionship with jars of pickles.

'Pickles again?' Rachel would laugh. 'Really, honey, you gotta stop it with the pickles – there's no way we can get through them this fast.'

'I know,' I'd tell her.

'It's getting so there's no room for anything else in the kitchen,' she'd say.

'I know,' I'd tell her.

'Soon we'll run out of space completely,' she'd say. 'And what'll happen then?'

'I don't know,' I'd tell her. 'I just don't know.'

This morning, after adding the compass to my collection of items, I considered leaving for seven and a half minutes – according to the old-timey fake station clock that ticks away too loudly on our wall. Then I shut the case back in the wardrobe, took my coat from the hook in the hall, and stepped out into the city.

I tell Rachel I'm spending my days job-hunting. Not that I particularly need to work – she has family money and anyway earns more than enough for two people with no dependants. But I want to be able to contribute. She nods seriously and understandingly whenever I tell her this. Rachel is one of those individuals who is consciously trying very hard to be a good person. Not that she isn't naturally a good person. It's just that she's always making such an effort at it, if you know what I mean.

'Of course,' she says to me whenever I tell her I want to start working too. 'Of course I understand.'

So I tell her I'm job-hunting. And it doesn't feel like a lie. More a simplification. Because what I'm doing, walking around these streets all day, tossing bits of stale bagel to the birds in Central Park, looking in windows, picking up flyers –

...STOP_MOTION: A 21st Century Dance Odyssey by Wendell Brown – FAT

CATS SHOULD NOT HAVE NINE LIVES: MAKE WALL STREET PAY –
space vs. inspace: photography of the new mind – Cleaner: reliable, punctual
and discreet, $7.50 an hour, call 504-7443 for more info!...

– it all feels like some kind of unnamed equivalent for job-hunting, if you understand what I mean. As if I'm hunting for something here, definitely, but what it is exactly, I'm not sure. And I think I'll know it when I see it, I do – but then I guess most people with a feeling of searching must think something like that or they simply wouldn't bother at all.

So today, anyway, I did what I mostly always do. I wandered down Columbus Avenue and bought a copy of every English newspaper – bar *The Daily Mail*, of course, and the crappier tabloids, which I basically don't count as newspapers anyway considering they contain no actual news – that I could find at the newsstand at the corner of West 89th. You know the one – nestled right alongside one of those spindly trees New York insists on lining its roads with. But I should say – it's been surprising to me, really quite surprising – this New York thing of having newsvendors set up on practically every street corner. In London, you see, we seem to have fallen out of love with print media so completely we'd rather walk the streets staring down at smartphone screens while reliable news sources go bankrupt around us than buy a paper. Seriously, you should look down the middle of a Northern Line carriage on a weekday evening. There are just rows and rows of us, all staring down, all silent, all transfixed by screens, going home. But the situation doesn't seem to be nearly so bad here, if the number of newsstands is anything to go by, not nearly as bad at all. Or maybe it's just that struggling newsvendors are allowed to take out bigger loans. Anyway, this particular guy I go to, this guy on West 89th who I get my papers from in the mornings – he's a total Anglophile. And he just loves London – hence his being (or so he proudly claims) the only newsstand in Manhattan to carry up-to-date copies of all the English newspapers – even the aforementioned crappy ones. Hence me actually having to make the decision to avoid them. It almost feels like being home.'

Silvia Kwon is the recipient of the Malcolm Bradbury Memorial Scholarship 2017/18. She holds a first degree in Art History. Her fiction has appeared in *Kill Your Darlings* and her non-fiction in leading newspapers. She has been shortlisted for a Varuna Fellowship and longlisted for the Fish Story Prize.

Sien and Vincent
Extract from a novel

Sien and Vincent explores the love affair between Vincent Van Gogh and his model/girlfriend Sien Hoornik, who was a prostitute. They lived together in The Hague between 1882–83.

She now specialised in 'the French way'; it sounded elegant and sophisticated, but really, it was just another way to screw with your mouth; and the mouth was ageless – thank God – for, at almost forty, her other instrument was as flaccid as the leather bellows of an accordion.

She didn't understand why many of the girls scorned fellatio. If they'd experienced the pregnancies she'd endured, she was sure they'd feel differently. It was true: many of her clients were no longer rakish; indeed, they were almost jaundiced-frail with prune-shrivelled cocks, but their need for pleasure was beyond their power to deny. Men with top hats and those with wooden shoes were reduced by it in equal measure.

On this evening, after four French-styles consecutively, her tongue was heavy and tired, her throat ragged and swollen. So, when there was a knock on her door, she hesitated. She knew it was late, close to midnight. She could tell by the quietening streets: the bustling city was in retreat.

She paused with her hand on the door handle, rubbing her finger and thumb on the smooth, worn timber. Could she do one more? Yes, just one more, because tomorrow was Sunday and it was always slow on the holy day, for the men, spooked by the priest's sermon, imposed a moratorium on their urges.

He was neither young nor old. He wore a crumpled grey suit, his restless fingers spinning the brim of his black felt hat. 'I was told you do the French way,' he blurted out.

She nodded, taking in his dark beard and darting eyes that, in a disquieting skitter, managed to both push away and pull at her gaze, betraying an inner struggle. He needed loosening up, that was clear. She guessed his wife already had six or seven and refused to let him touch her; besides, he probably couldn't bear it anyway, to see his wife's fair face at the end of his cock.

She stood aside to let him in. 'You can put your hat there,' she said, pointing to a hook next to the door. 'You'll be more comfortable too if you take off your jacket.'

He did as he was told, but mindfully, as if he were just learning how to move his limbs.

'Your first time?'

He took a step back before answering, 'Yes.'

'Well, some like to sit and some like to lie on their back. Take your pick; whatever you like.' She moved the chair from the wall to the middle of the room, then glanced at the narrow iron bed.

'I think I'll just sit.'

'It's fifty cents.'

'Yes, I have it here.' He searched his trouser pocket and took out the coin. Unsure whether to offer it to her, he held it awkwardly in his palm until she pointed her chin at the bed-table. 'Just over there.'

He was certainly a fresh one; usually they waited until the end.

Still, he stood there.

'Well, I can't do anything if your trousers are on.'

'Yes, yes, of course.' His hands quickly reached for his braces. They slid off his shoulders, releasing his trousers to his ankles, and he duck-walked to the chair.

She shook her head, amused.

Then he sat in his drawers and waited.

She sighed. 'It would be a good idea if you took it out as well.'

She was relieved to note that it was a slender, two-finger size for some of the larger ones made her gag. She cleared her throat and went to work, kneeling on a small rug.

Some only dribbled in her mouth but he exploded. The fresh oyster-slick discharge was warm and sour, with a brackish bitterness that was common to all men. But this one also had an iron-tinged flavour that reminded her of a blacksmith's workshop, followed by a faint taste of mouldy cheese. She spat it into a bowl. She knew some women swallowed because it made them less hungry but she could not stomach it.

As he dressed, she said, 'I noticed you have paint on the back of your hands. Are you an artist?'

He snapped on his braces and spun around. His countenance had changed; his eyes were relaxed but alert, his skin vivid as if fresh air had blasted through his pores.

'Yes,' he replied, raising his brows.

'I lived with one once, a few years ago, in The Hague,' she said, matter-of-factly.

His eyes lit up. 'One of The Hague School painters?'

'No, he knew them, but no. His name was Van Gogh. Vincent.'

He cocked his head, curious. 'You said you lived with him? And your name?'

She nodded, wiping her mouth with a flannel towel. 'It's Sien.'

'Well, Sien, I'm sure you know that his family is very well known in the art world,' said the artist.

She read his implication: how had she, a prostitute, ended up living with a gentleman artist? It was true: their love should never have happened. That it had still astounded her.

'Yes, his uncle owned many galleries throughout Europe,' she said. 'And another uncle was an admiral in the navy...' Rankled by thoughts of Vincent's family, she gripped the back of the chair too tight and made it rock.

'Ah, quite an illustrious Dutch family,' the artist remarked. 'I only knew of him at Café Tambourine. A few of his paintings were displayed there; I admired his treatment of flowers.'

So, he'd ended up in Paris, she mused. The French prostitutes; they had spoken fondly of that gay city, how much more delightful the nightlife, how much more handsome the men. Yet, she'd always imagined him in Amsterdam, a successful artist, married to a woman from his world, with children, living in a grand house overlooking a canal.

The artist continued. 'Of course, his brother is a well-known art dealer there. Did you know him, too?'

'I remember Theo,' she said flatly. The dapperly suited and pomaded young man with pin-sharp eyes and a crimped mouth that did not move once during their meeting, while Vincent's was chatter-busy, doing the talk of more than two men.

'They were close, from what I heard. They were apparently quite a presence at the dance halls too,' the artist said, chortling before coughing into his hand.

She bristled at this news. He'd obviously done well without her, gallivanting around Paris with his brother. It was always that way for him. For all his talk of suffering, what did he really know about it?

'How long did you two live together?' the artist asked, a smirk playing around the corners of his mouth.

'Nearly two years. I sat for him as a model.'

He traced her from head to foot, eyes sparkling. 'He drew you?'

'Yes, many times.'

Scratchings, he'd called them, their apartment a small art gallery. How many did he do in those years? Hundreds? At least.

His brows pinched and his expression clouded, preoccupied by some thought.

'So, was it all right?' she asked, flicking her eyes towards his groin. She didn't want her reputation tarnished; it was competitive amongst the women.

He nodded, but absent-mindedly; only half-listening. Then his face slackened. 'I should tell you, he died two months ago.'

The towel in her hand dropped to the floor. 'Dead?'

'Yes, a gunshot.' A pause. 'Self-inflicted, I'm afraid. In France.'

The room slipped from her vision as scenery from the window of a train, but Vincent flared in her memory – too bright, hot, painful, a high summer sun.

'Are you all right?' the artist asked.

She doll-flopped on the bed, her body both heavy and empty. 'It can't be true,' she said, her voice thin. 'By his own hand? A gun?' He'd had his demons, she knew, but the man she'd lived with in The Hague seven years ago had possessed an unyielding will for life.

He nodded.

She gulped a mouthful of jenever from her flask on the bedside table, shuddering as the fiery bittersweet drink jolted her. She shook her head and spoke firmly. 'But it's so unlike him...' Hadn't he, when she threatened to throw herself into the river, turned angrily to her and said, 'You can never give in to despair. Never. Do you hear? Suffering is the gift of life.'

She offered the flask to the artist, who accepted it and took a swig.

As tears pooled, she said, 'You must tell me, tell me everything you know.' She'd spent these past seven years trying to forget him, but now a torrent of contradictory feelings – anger, regret, love – flooded her.

The artist sat across from her. 'I'm afraid I can't tell you too much. I know he left Paris to go to the south of France. Someone mentioned Arles, but I'm not sure. I do know there was some trouble at Café Tambourine.'

'Trouble?' This did not surprise her.

'Yes, with the owner, about his paintings; and the last time I saw him he didn't look well. But Paris can do that to you if you're not careful. There, the absinthe... well, one could say it's as famous as the city.'

'So, he sold his art? He was successful in Paris?' she asked, her voice eager but also hesitant. Did she want to know?

He shook his head. 'Well, no, I haven't heard talk of his art selling as such, but an influential critic wrote a very good review earlier this year, and it looked promising for him.'

'You have the article?'

'Yes, at home.'

'Will you bring it?' she implored. She was surprised by her hunger for his news – though unsure what good it would do her. 'She unlocked her clasped hands and, wiping the damp corners of her eyes on her sleeve, rasped, 'I won't charge you next time you come.'

The artist leaned forward. 'All right; but tell me, was he a client? Is that how you met?'

For many years, she had been unable to speak of him. She, too, had eventually fled The Hague. But she realised now it had made no difference: he was still with her, in the painful and useless memories she carried within.

'No, it wasn't quite like that. But I wish I'd never met him.'

Louise Lamb was raised in England and New Jersey. She holds a BA in English and Film from Trinity College, Dublin and has lived in Ireland since graduating. Louise writes science fiction, fantasy and horror. She is currently working on a weird fiction novel.

The Breach
Excerpt from a novel

Rebecca waited for the shuttle: a wicker basket that descended out of the yellow smog. She had wrapped her body in leather and wool despite the greenhouse heat. Her turned-up collar made her breath wet.

She stepped inside the basket and pulled a gas mask from its peg. Hundreds of faces had breathed into it. Slow inhalation, slow exhalation. The basket jerked and began to rise, carrying her out of her city into the one above.

She entered the smog, a thick layer of pollution that lingered between the cities. She could smell the poison air despite her mask's charcoal filters. It pinched the exposed skin between her gloves and her cuffs, and pushed against her goggles. She waited, encased. Inhalation. Exhalation.

When she emerged on the other side of the acid cloud, she had to blink against the bright light. Sun snatched every part of the spectrum, revealing the underside of the sky city. Tangled pipes and thick veins of copper wiring ran, as arteries, into its belly. Zeppelins held it suspended, jumbling in the wind. The place that was powered. The place that was provided for. The place with the better half of the sky.

Rebecca could feel a storm on the air. The zeppelins would soon screech with effort, driving against the wind to keep the city from breaking its moorings. To keep it from hurtling over the ocean or deep inland to places so sparsely polluted that people would be able to see the green fields below them.

Rebecca removed the gas mask and stepped out of the shuttle.

The city was a series of islands, linked by swinging bridges. It looked like a crazed circus had been catapulted into the heavens. Everything avoided heaviness. The streets were grated bronze. The buildings were canvas big tops in pale blue, green, and pink.

Even the people had waned thin, and wore white overcoats against the altitude's icy gales. They were jewelled: dyeing their short hair bright colours better to catch the light. Rebecca was a brown and solid creature beside them, winding her way to an access ladder and climbing past the starved, regal crowds.

When she qualified as a zeppelin engineer, the guild had given her wax-wrapped packages: the mangled innards of fish or over-plumped pigeon.

The protein gave her the strength she needed to navigate the city's ladders. Arriving to fix, to repair, to examine, to maintain.

She grew warmer beneath her jacket, and paused for four breaths before climbing again. If she let herself sweat she would be sorry for it. She would shiver and long for the trapped heat on the ground. A place as warm as the touch of skin on skin.

Rebecca clung to a rope bridge and inched toward the zeppelin cabin at its far end. The cabin door swung open and a young woman leaned out.

'Hi Piper,' Rebecca called to her sister, raising her voice over the creaking cables.

Piper beckoned her inside and shut the door. At the last minute the air caught it and slammed it closed, rattling the glass in its window. Rebecca stamped her feet, urging warmth into them, and unzipped her jacket. Piper had cranked the air vents open, welcoming the hot fumes from her foremost engine.

'You took your time getting here,' Piper said. Her hair was darker than her sister's, plaited at the back of her skull.

Rebecca smiled and ignored the comment. 'I hear you're having some engine trouble,' she said.

'You could put it that way.'

Piper had a habit of circling her words, reaching the end of a point only enthusiastically to begin it again. She began to talk about her problem, misusing vocabulary from her sister's textbooks.

As Piper spoke, Rebecca peered out the windows at the relevant propellers. The cabin was half glass and Rebecca could see the pilots in the neighbouring zeppelins. She bent to find the tools she would need in her backpack and Piper trailed off.

'You don't need everything?' Piper asked.

'I don't think so,' Rebecca said, clipping her selection onto her belt. 'Probably best if I just take a look.'

Piper took an audible breath, then nodded. 'You're right. I don't even know why I'm telling you all this stuff.' She slid a golden lever on the console, and the engines shuddered into silence. The ship bobbed in the air. 'Be careful,' she said. 'Is there anything you need me to do here?'

Rebecca wondered if Piper meant for her to be careful of herself or of the machine.

*

The faulty motor was housed in the port wing power car. To reach it, Rebecca would need to climb along the zeppelin's belly, thousands of feet above the ground. She tugged experimentally on her safety harness, kicked one leg over the rail, and lowered herself into open air.

The zeppelin was pierced with metal handholds that ran front to back. Rebecca hung from them, as if from a ladder turned parallel to the earth. She crawled feet first, feeling the chill air against her eyes.

The progress was slow. Every time she looked out between the airships, Rebecca saw the storm-grey cloud coming closer.

She stopped every few rungs to move her safety clips along. There was ice on the dark metal of the brackets. When she cast her eyes down, she was unable to see her city through the opaque smog.

By the time she reached the power car Rebecca was sweating, and she knew she would be cold by sunset. The cab was packed with machinery, and smelt of shearing iron. Rebecca crouched, put her face close to the sleeping motor, and began to talk herself through its difficulties. She laid her fingers on each part as she went.

'Looks good, seems fine. You could use a clean but I think you're doing OK otherwise. Oh, you need some help here, don't you.'

She found evidence of her sister's repairs. They were clumsy, but they were the only things keeping the ship running. Rebecca tried not to think of Piper hanging from those handholds, twisting to check how far she had left to travel.

The day wore into evening as Rebecca made her adjustments, sliding pieces together and replacing as much as she could. Squinting in the darkness, she propped the door open, needing the last rays of sunlight to continue her work. Still, as she made progress she found further faults. The issues Piper knew about were only the beginning: each repair revealed daisy chains of problems.

Rebecca rubbed a hand across her face, turning again to look at the open door. There must be enough light. There was so much she could still do. She leaned to the side so that her shadow wouldn't fall on the engine and tried to keep working. Her eyes were an inch from the metal and still she couldn't make it out fully.

It was too late, she had lost the light, and as the storm pulled closer, the engine was not fixed.

Rebecca's return was difficult. She was buffeted by the storm's first lashes, and when she reached the cabin she found her shoulders had seized. Piper already had milk on the hot plate, and stirred pieces of dark chocolate into it with a small spoon. Outside, electric bulbs made the tents glow in the darkness.

'You must be freezing,' Piper said, offering Rebecca a mug. 'Did you have any luck back there?'

'I made some headway. It should be fine,' Rebecca said.

Piper bit her lip. They both knew the storm would trap her, and she would have to drive hard to counteract the wind. She needed the engine to work.

'Are you sure it's good enough, that it'll hold?' Piper asked.

'I wouldn't be leaving if I wasn't sure. It'll be fine, Piper. Give it a try now, we can double check,' Rebecca said. She kept her tone light. After the storm, when everything was calmer, she would return to finish the job. For now, she thought, it was better not to worry her little sister with the details.

Piper turned to the controls and Rebecca felt the engine's low vibrations in her boots. Piper didn't smile. She was focused, careful not to unbalance anything as she tested the responsiveness.

'It's better already, isn't it?' Rebecca asked.

'It seems to be,' Piper admitted. Rebecca watched her sister for a long moment, both of them reluctant to part. Eventually Piper nodded. 'You better be getting home before the wind gets any stronger.'

'You're right. I'll see you soon then.'

As Rebecca swung back across the bridge she thought of her sister's face, lined with worry. She couldn't blame her. If the machine gave out, both cities could be in trouble. An entire population reliant on the pilots to fight the wind, to keep everything in place. Rebecca tried to remember the parts that were still weak, imagining the havoc they would cause if one of them were to give out. It should hold, she told herself. Piper should be fine.

Rebecca shivered and set the shuttle moving before she caught the gas mask, only strapping it into place moments before she sank, feet first, into the smog.

Ayanna Gillian Lloyd is a writer from Trinidad & Tobago. She has been published in *The Caribbean Writer*, *Moko Magazine*, *Small Axe: A Caribbean Journal of Criticism* and shortlisted for the Wasafiri New Writing Prize. She lives in Norwich and is working on her first novel. Find her at www. ayannagillianlloyd.com.

The Gatekeepers
Excerpt from a novel

*In Port Angeles magic, myth and violence are part of everyday life. The heart
of the city is a graveyard that holds the long dead and new mysteries. It is here
that two people meet and fall in love, even as bodies go missing and strange
characters appear. As their destinies intertwine, they find that their relationship
is more than flesh, and holds the secret to the fate of their crumbling city.*

—

It had been raining for three days in Morne Marie. Yejide sat at the window
of her room on the third floor of the house, watched the sky empty itself
into the valley and waited for her mother, Petronella, to die. It wouldn't be
long now. For as long as there had been stories told about the women in
her family, death always came on the third day of the storm.

Most of the villagers would worry about houses, livestock and crops –
living with a river meant the constant knowledge that she gives, and she
takes away – but those who had lived in Morne Marie longest knew the
truth. They knew just as well as Yejide did that this was no ordinary storm.
There was something about the intensity of the rain, the way everything
seemed to pause and wait like the earth had stopped spinning. She couldn't
see them, but she was certain that in each house in the valley below, there
were elders gathered, candles being lit, and prayers being whispered for
death to come to the house on the hill, so the villagers would all be spared.

There had been little sleep for anyone as the household kept vigil at her
mother's deathbed. It seemed as though even the floorboards whispered
the questions that had been on all of their minds: when will Petronella call
for Yejide? Will she pass on the legacy before the storm breaks?

Waiting was nothing new to Yejide. She had spent most of her life
waiting for her mother – waiting for her to come, waiting for her to leave,
for her sharp reprimand for some slight or slip, for her to notice that she'd
kept her clothes nice and neat for church, that she'd managed to help her
grandmother set the table without breaking a single thing – waiting for
anything to indicate that her mother had noticed that she had a daughter
at all.

Yejide rubbed her eyes. Since the wind had set up and the first few fat
raindrops began to pound the roof she had been tossing and turning under

the mosquito netting that hung over her bed, its white gauze softening the room in dusk light. She wasn't allowed into Petronella's room until sent for and between the waiting, the rain and the white gauze, it was hard for her to know whether she was asleep or awake.

On the first day, she thought her dead aunt Geraldine, wearing Petronella's clothes, had brought her a cup of tea and left it at her bedside. She had almost been able to smell the bitter turmeric root and feel the heat of the steam rising from the cup. On the second day, she had thought her old friend Seema had been in the bed next to her, stroking her hair.

But now in the soft early morning light of the third day, her mother dying down the corridor, all she could think of was her Granny Catherine who had died years before with the last great storm. Every Sunday after church if Yejide had been very good, hadn't messed up her dress and hadn't asked too many questions, Granny Catherine would tell the story about the world before time, of how death came to Morne Marie.

The story told how long ago, before the settlement, before the quarries, before even their house stood on the hill, when the forest was so thick that no man could cross it, Morne Marie was home to only the animals. But the animals that made their home there were not like animals we see now, oh no! Catherine would spread her arms wide. The ocelots were as big as tigers, the deer ran so fast that no man could catch them even if one dared to enter the forest to hunt them, and the green parrots that flew overhead and sang of the coming of the dusk were as big as the blood-red ibis that ruled the skies in the swamplands. Granny Catherine said the animals could talk to each other – yes, just like I am talking now, and chucked Yejide under her chin – and they built a mighty city in the forest.

But the city of the forest was not like our city now, nothing like Port Angeles at all with its crumbling concrete and asphalt to choke the roads so the rain couldn't meet its sister, the river underground. The city in the forest had no buildings and no boundaries and no gates and all the animals lived together without territory to guard and borders to mind.

But one day, a cunning warrior from the world of men wandered into the forest. He saw that it was full of animals to hunt and fruit to eat. He only saw the trees for the houses that he could build from them, and he only saw the land for what he could take from it, and although the animals tried to talk to him and tell him that there was so much more there than what he could see, he did not know their language and could not understand them.

The warrior brought more warriors and with the warriors came farmers, and with the farmers came builders, and with the builders came priests, and with the priests came governors, and with the governors came death.

'But the animals fought them, right?' Yejide loved this part. She would think of the sharp teeth of the ocelots and the tight grip of the macajuel that could suffocate a man in its coils and couldn't believe that humans with just two legs, very small teeth and no poison at all could ever defeat the wild animals of the forest.

Catherine would look down at her and frown, 'Who telling the story, you or me?' and wait for Yejide to settle into silence. Of course, the animals fought! And the war raged for a long time with losses on both sides. Then the animals made a mighty stand. The quarry you see there – and she would point out the window to the hills – was the site of a battle so fierce and so bloody that it left scars on the mountains.

Wounded, the forest went into mourning and this brought the longest dry season ever in Morne Marie. The rivers hid in the earth and the forest wilted. The ocelots shrank to the size of house cats, the howler monkeys grew timid, and the deer and manicou and lappe who had lived in peace before suddenly began to look at each other and see food. The warriors too had suffered losses for no one – neither man nor animal – could survive when nature decided to withhold its bounty.

Then one day, when all were weary, a great storm descended on the forest. The men and animals rejoiced to see the rivers rise again, and the forest drink deeply of the rain. The storm raged for three days and three nights. But time wasn't like we measure time now. Catherine would point to the old grandfather clock in the corner. This was time before clocks when a tree could reach full-grown in a day and a boy could grow to manhood in a night. This storm was longer and fiercer than any of the animals had ever seen.

Now, the green parrots – and here Catherine would pinch Yejide's lips together to stop her from giggling – you know the ones who cackle and sing and chatter plenty just like you? Well, they were wiser than any of the animals gave them credit for, flighty and happy as they were. The parrots watched the rain and watched the hills and watched the rivers and watched the animals and watched the armies of men gathered in all their numbers and held a secret council. At the council's end, they split and divided their number into two. One half flew to the east and the other half flew to the west.

The parrots that flew to the west shrank and became the small green parrots we see today, the ones that sing and fly toward the setting of the sun. The parrots that flew east toward the sunrise turned their green feathers shiny black and curved their beaks into hooks. They released one great song before they sprouted grey collars around their necks which silenced their throats, so they could never sing again.

'Do you know what they became, Yejide?' Catherine would look down at her and smile.

'Corbeaux!' Yejide had loved getting the right answer. No matter how many times she heard the story, knowing the answer always made her feel grown-up and very important.

They became corbeaux with black wings so wide that they darkened the land below. When the change was complete they felt their bellies grow hungry for flesh. They began to devour the dead animals who were once their friends and the slain men who were once their enemies.

The living looked on in horror to see the devouring of the dead but the corbeaux knew they were charged with a sacred duty. They knew what the other animals did not: that all things must die and that the forest was infinitely powerful, more so than the animals that reigned there and the men who had come to rule there could ever understand. They knew that balance must be kept. And so, they did their work. They waited for the dead and watched over the carcasses and consumed the flesh. No one else understood that in their bellies souls of the dead were transformed and released.

And so, on the third day, the rains ceased. But the corbeaux were despised and feared in the forest by men and animals alike, and over time everyone forgot that the ending of the storm happened with their birth.

'So, who win the war then, granny? The men or the animals?' Yejide would ask.

'Chile, you must learn to figure out when the telling part of a story done,' Catherine would say. Then she would smile and smooth down the green dress that had flared up and bunched around Yejide's waist and send her on her way. 'Right. Now make sure and put that dress away. Hang it on the back of the chair in my room. Don't let me come and find that you haven't. Your shoes too. Go on. Then find Seema and go outside and count the lizards before your mother come home.'

Yejide thought of the years in between Granny Catherine's first telling of the story and the last. It wasn't until she was too tall for little girl dresses, was grown enough to sit beside her grandmother instead of on her lap that she had asked the most important question. She never thought to ask Granny Catherine when she was alive how old she had been, she had first asked it of her mother, and there was no way Yejide would have asked Petronella how old she had been when she had asked it of Catherine. 'Granny, we here in Morne Marie since before it had a name. Who side we was on? The men or the animals?' As Yejide listened for a break in the rain she could almost hear Granny Catherine's voice on the wind, 'We, my darling, are only and always on the side of the dead. We are the corbeaux.'

Philly Malicka grew up in Essex and has a degree in English literature from Oxford University. Her first novel, *All Along of You*, has been longlisted for the Bridport Prize. She lives in London and works in publishing.

All Along of You
Extract from a novel

'I know it's open,' Mary said to me, over her bare shoulder.

I was trying to impress her by standing back on the cobbled street and taking in the building, sizing up all the swirls of Baroque architecture like I understood what I was looking at.

With one hand on the handle, she threw the whole length of her long body against the small wooden door. It held fast, but the crash she made disturbed a scatter of pigeons into the pink sky above us, disturbed my nerves too. This was different from my parents' church at home, chapels like this had to be tiptoed around, revered. As she flapped at the handle and pushed the door with her foot I thought, *forgive us our trespasses,* while I glanced up and down Via Giulia. I would get used to this feeling as Mary and I became better friends; the embarrassment I felt when she was impatient with something; the physical way she would vent her frustrations, how quickly she could turn vandal. She was the richest yob I'd ever met.

When the door finally buckled we were hit by a wave of damp cool air. She took hold of my hand, crushing my knuckles as she guided me through the nave, towards the front of the dim chapel, past rows of seated nuns, faces silver as moons, thumbs tucked up into the corners of their eyes as they crooked over themselves in prayer. Quickly, we crossed the front of the church, straight past the craggy gold altar, taking giant exaggerated steps. We laughed loudly, because we didn't care if we were noticed; we wanted to be noticed. That was unspoken between us. All those dried up religious women, they had to know what they were missing.

We left the main church on the left side and she took me down a flight of steps to a new room, much darker, without pews or organ pipes or basins of holy water. This place was small and square and without windows. It smelt damp and mossy, like it had been dredged out of a riverbank. I could hear the sound of water trickling down walls and it was collecting in small puddles on the dirty floor. Then Mary spoke.

'La Santa Maria dell'Orazione e Morte', she said in a faultless accent, twirling her wrists and gesturing like an Italian *Signora.* 'Isn't it freaky!'

I turned away from her and looked around. At one end was a modest altar or perhaps just an old shelf where a cross was propped up against a wall, illuminated by amber lights. It gave out a hollow glow, casting no other light on the rest of the room. I had to walk right up to the cross and then wheel about to inspect the cabinets on the side of the room before I could deduce the nature of the objects surrounding me. The room was packed full of human skulls.

'This – is like a crypt?' My voice came out like a hiss.

'*Certo*! Technically it's called an ossuary.'

'Holy fuck!'

She laughed, then hushed me, taking hold of me by my elbow.

We inspected the skulls together. They were lined up obediently in the brown cabinets, as dusty and congruent as old medicine bottles. In the first cabinet, the one nearest the altar, the skulls still had their jaws attached and inanely grinned at us.

'What did these people do? Were they criminals?'

'Some of them, probably. I think the rest were just dead bodies without families to claim them. The Members of the church collected up all their bones and left them here. The closest thing to a proper burial, I think.'

We moved along the wall and she showed me rows and rows of skulls where a date had been etched into the ridges of the brow bone.

'No name. No identity. Only the date they were found.'

On the top of the next cabinet was a speckled plaque, which read 'Il Tevere'. It housed all the skulls of those bodies who'd been drowned or discarded in the River Tiber. Mary showed me the craniums that had holes blown right through the front of them and then a couple with holes in the side where the bullet had curved on its forward trajectory and left out of the temple, like the side door to the church, which we had come through. But it was those skulls, which were cracked and damaged, and showed evidence of blunt trauma that interested her specifically. She told me as she chatted that she liked to imagine how it happened, how the blow was delivered, what the poor victim might have seen as they died. But Mary also valued the cracks in the skulls on some visual, decorative level. She took her finger and traced along the fissures in the bone admiringly, the way each crack led onto another. The lines were connected but somehow wild and unstable, like territory markings on an old globe.

As she stroked the notches in the bone, I let out a deep breath. I tried to cover it up, as if I was sighing in awe at the expired lives of all these yellow skulls, when really I was thinking about her, the recent feeling of her fingers, as she'd held mine. I tried to focus on the cleaved triangular holes in the skulls where the nose used to be, but something about its shape made me think of the nuns upstairs. This confused me, slightly shamed me, so I turned away from the cabinet and pretended to search for my sketchbook, ramming my hands deep into my bag.

'I've noticed this about you,' she said. 'You're always sketching.'

'That's what I'm here to learn.'

'It's a bit obsessive.'

Now I was sketching, Mary behaved as if the skulls no longer interested her. This was something I'd also noticed at the school, the sideways glimpses she gave to others' work as we painted the same model. Working communally made her agitated and competitive. She leant against a wall and began scrolling through her cheap Italian phone.

'Do you think about your own mortality?' she asked, after a pause.

'Not my own,' I said. The question seemed naive, like we were ten year olds at a sleepover. 'Sometimes my parents'.'

'Uch.'

She made a choking noise.

'There's a sick thought, my own mother's skull.'

'Not true,' I tried to counter. 'I went to Lawrence's lecture. I saw her with you at the party, she's beautiful.'

'So everyone says.'

'So, I'm sure your mother would make a lovely skull.'

At that she went silent and all I could hear was the bleeping of her phone. She loved to do this, engage you in conversation then duck out suddenly, leaving you hanging on the sound of your own ludicrous words, which without her responses to frame them, lost all meaning. Later on, I would learn just to repeat myself, in a smaller voice. *A lovely skull.*

But then she spoke up again, abruptly.

'My mother saw me with Lawrence, at the party. She walked in on us together in the cloakroom upstairs. And she did nothing.'

'Lawrence? As in, *our* Lawrence?' I said, feigning confusion and squinting towards the skulls.

'I know you saw us too,' she said, in a flat voice.

I carried on drawing, not wanting to look at her. I didn't want to be reminded of her dazed expression when I stood on the marble staircase and saw them both stumble out of the coat room. Her falling bra strap and dirty blonde hair all matted. That appalling sight of Lawrence, the director of the course, a man well into his sixties, nuzzling at her long neck and guiding her forward towards the stairs with his hand on the small of her back; the thought of his broad hands, raw from turps, cuticles crusted with acrylic, chancing all over her body.

'Can you believe that?' she said, her voice quavering. 'She didn't do anything. She didn't say anything. My own mother.'

'Why should she do anything?' I said, staring forward. 'Is it her business who you're with?'

'I wasn't getting with Lawrence out of choice, Gus, and Mum could tell that. It was obvious.' She paused, as I turned to look at her face, her symmetrical features seemed warped and stricken. She shook her head and whispered, 'He thought he'd locked the door.'

I stared at her, trying to gauge the full measure of what she was telling me. The gloom of the crypt and the whole scene around us began to fall away, as I watched her mouth opening and closing, the quick rising of her shoulders. I reached out for her hand.

'Mum witnessed the whole thing,' she said, as she moved her hand away from me, pulling her shorts up over the flesh on her hips by the belt-holes. 'Mum must have heard me, or seen me fighting him. But she just closed the door.'

Sitting here, almost three years later, I try and reach for the nearest consecutive detail in our story. But all I can remember is our ending. The last time I saw Mary.

It was almost a year ago now in south London, the day MG was arrested. I was early for my session so I sat reading some of the literature on the kerb opposite her house. The pavement warmed me through the seat of my jeans and I tilted my head to the sun, unaware of the police car a metre or so away from her front gate. Very little time seemed to pass between the moment MG's front door opened and the next when I recognised the outline of Mary running up the hill towards me.

She had grown a little heavier in the years since Rome but her stride was still quick. She seemed to possess the same force of the girl who had thrown her bodyweight against the door to enter the church on that day in Rome. For a moment she looked graceful, racing towards me in the bright orange light. Then she opened her mouth and began swearing, a torrent of Brixton-borrowed filth. When she reached the police car she started kicking at it wildly, a spray of limbs, one foot permanently off the ground and denting the bodywork like a dancing Shiva.

They should be arresting her, I remember thinking. The police will release MG and turn on Mary instead, which will be just and fair because look at her, she's wild, she's a vandal. But the police officers, man and woman, just started the engine up and let Mary continue. Back when I was still at school, I'd watch the police clear a group of travellers from some local farmland. Keeping a firm line, their Jeeps and tractors tore up the turf, overturning mobile homes, liberating horses and dogs. I recognised their expressions from that day; identically tightened as they ignored the abuse. The police car moved off then at speed, tyres crackling against the dry asphalt.

Mary was panting when she walked over to where I was standing. I can still recall the shock of being acknowledged, as if I'd been watching the scene unfold in a film or a dream or some high up ledge where no one could notice me.

'This is all my fault,' she said. Her blue eyes had darkened and now seemed as grey as the road we were standing on. 'My family set this up. And MG knew about it. She warned me. She said she was being watched.'

I murmured something back in response. Maybe I told her not to worry. I reached for her hand and got her fingers instead. Like a baby, I gripped them hard, but it was too late. She had already slipped off.

Senica Maltese is a Canadian writer. In 2016, she received UEA's North American Bursary Scholarship. She has a BA in Writing and English Literature from the University of Victoria, where she served on *The Malahat Review*'s Fiction Board. Senica was recently accepted onto UEA's PhD in Creative and Critical Writing.

Edge of the World

After a few at St Vincent and Urbane, Jocasta ropes you into going to one of those cuddle orgies at the Island Community Centre. You're drinking Dark Matter, the only beer you will truly miss when you move to London, though you'll insist that, on a whole, BC craft beers are better than anything they've got in stupid, old Britain. Land of Beer, my ass, you will say, mostly when you are drunk, and missing home, and can't remember who told you that this was the Land of Beer in the first place.

It's your last night in Tofino, and Jocasta has stained her lips coral, just for you. Because you're tacky, she says. And like that sorta thing. That sorta thing being the Pacific, and sunsets. But she's the one tacky enough to jig her lipstick to your tastes, so you know that she'll miss you – that she doesn't think any of this is tacky at all, even though, probably, it is.

You've had about a pint and a half too many, considering it's only six and Jocasta's not likely to let you go until past midnight and there's an Air Canada seat with your name on it at nine sharp in the morning – and did you remember to pack all the things you can't leave behind? The French press you've had since you moved out of your mother's house in Montreal is tucked under your sweaters: a collection curated over five years on Vancouver Island, where the coffee's brewed strong and the sweaters are butt-ugly and smell of hemp. You've heard that the whole of Europe is *espresso, espresso, espresso* and the thought repulses you.

(Later, when you've met the first of many men that you would have liked to marry, he heckles you for loving the taste of mud, but you're stubborn and you'll brew your coffee like a Canadian the rest of your goddamn life.)

But what about the things that can't be packed? The places and the people. The whole great big Pacific.

Jocasta isn't sitting across from you anymore. She's standing with her denim jacket slung over her arm. She wipes lipstick from the edge of her mouth with a pinkie finger, then bends to slurp the last of her G&T. Orange smudges on the straw.

Come on, she says. We don't wanna miss the action.

Gulp your beer, apologise.

You're just a little distracted. You're afraid of change, and you don't like to meet new people. At twenty-two, you aren't sure how you've gotten this far – broadly speaking, like, in life – and, up until a few hours ago, you were convinced that the move wouldn't actually happen, that you'd spend the rest of your infinitesimal time-blip right here, within three hundred kilometres of the coastal city where you were born.

As far as you know, that may still be the case – though you hope, hope, hope it isn't. The plane could explode, you could lose your Visa, the university could call, say: Sorry, Big Mistake.

For you, everything seems likely, or unlikely, until it does, or doesn't, happen and you find your own mind exhausting.

Finish your drink, Jocasta says. It's cuddle time. She clicks her fingers in a brisk series of snaps and winks at you.

You feel like you've swallowed a gopher.

Down it with the last of your pint.

Say, I'm ready.

—

The Cuddle Assistant introduces himself as Justin-Still-In-Training and hands you a pink leaflet. Here are the rules, he says. It's all pretty basic: keep your clothes on and don't cuddle without consent. Always wait for a verbal 'yes' before you touch someone.

Justin-Still-In-Training doesn't speak like someone in training and you wonder if this is what he wants to be: a Cuddle Therapist, or something.

So, you say: Is this what you want to do with your life? and immediately feel like a philosophical ass-hat.

You'd like to explain how you're going through a quiet crisis of the self right now, but don't have the words or the follow-through to share this with a total stranger. Besides, the whole thing feels pretty dumb.

Justin-Still-In-Training blinks. I just wanna live, man.

Jocasta laughs. Don't we all, she says, and she seems genuinely happy. Also sad.

You nod, say: Sorry. What I mean, I guess, is do you believe in cuddles? Do you think they're therapeutic or whatever?

Justin-Still-In-Training smiles: an Island-Zen, forgiving smile. Man, it's whatever you make it.

You think: Whoa, that's probably true, not just of cuddles, but generally speaking. Of life.

As long as what you make it isn't sexual, Justin-Still-In-Training says. Because then we will kick you out.

—

The Cuddle Room is bit like the padded panic room you saw in a film once when you were twelve. Except that it's big and full of strangers in pyjamas. There are giant, blue pillows everywhere, and the cuddle-action has already begun. Cuddle-action, meaning thirty people between the ages of twenty and fifty clumped together in twos and threes, with the occasional singleton sprawled out on the floor.

Immediately, you know that you don't want to cuddle any of these fools; also, that they aren't fools, but you're grumpy and you hate team-building activities and trust games, and that's pretty much what this is.

You wonder: Why the hell would Jocasta bring me here?

Maybe she hates you, after all. Maybe this is one great, big fuck you for trying to leave her. Even though you say it's only for a couple of years and then you'll be back home; even though she says she'll come to visit you during your summer vacations – you suspect this change is something greater than either of you will articulate, that the two of you will become snagged in your own lives: that Justin-Still-In-Training will ask for Jocasta's number and take her to a nice dinner, something with kale and avocado and salmon, that in five years they will buy an apartment together in Victoria, and have a whole life you can't really be a part of.

But then Jocasta takes your hand and sits you down in a quiet spot by the window where you can hear the faint rattle of the ocean, that big Pacific blue, and she holds you.

Arathi Menon's first book *Leaving Home With Half A Fridge* was published by Pan Macmillan India (2015). *A Suitcase of Small Stories*, a short story, will be published in the UK (2018). She was longlisted for the Ivan Juritz prize (2018) and received a Highly Commendable mention at the FAB prize (Faber & Faber, 2018). She is the recipient of the International Office Excellence Scholarship from UEA. Currently, she is working on a novel and a children's book.

On Wednesdays We Have Spinach
An excerpt from a novel

Her breasts hung low, pointing towards the terracotta flooring, cool under her still pedicured feet. 'Not that low', she told herself fiercely but she couldn't escape the memory of the pencil test. A lifetime ago, when she was in school, they had all gathered in the common loo and quickly stripped off their shirts, petticoats and bras. Six sets of breasts were reflected in a mirror still sprayed with little flecks of toothpaste from the morning.

It was Radha who took out the black and red striped Natraj pencil, and stuck it under her left breast. It immediately fell, clattering and rolling into the corner where loose strands of hair had collected, coiled into each other, mixed-up, identities forgotten. She promised them with a maniacal glee that a time would come when their breasts would flop down and they could hold one, two, three pencils, tucked under their bending folds, 'That's when you know you are old, when nobody will look at you.'

For years Ira would do the pencil test. Sometimes, when she didn't have a pencil, she'd use a toothbrush. Once she even tried it with Adi's razor, which fell on her thigh, nicking her skin before it hit the floor. She smeared the blood with her finger and didn't wash it off till the next day.

Ira cupped a breast each in her palms and lifted them. Did it make a difference? Would nobody look at her now? She hadn't looked at herself in the mirror for a long time. Her stomach wasn't flat, a small speed bump lay across it. Her pubic hair was overgrown, with tendrils shooting out into the air. She touched herself, it was so rough. Did she need to use conditioner?

Her legs still looked good. Beautifully shaped and toned, they at least pretended she worked out. She moved her shoulders slightly, bits of her hair swished back and forth. She couldn't look at her face. Instead, she turned towards the ventilator, three feet above her head, and opened her mouth to suck in the sun. A tiny gecko sat, flicking his tongue. She dared him to exchange bodies.

When she had removed her clothes she had folded them neatly and placed them one on top of another, a tiny mountain for an ant. Now she snatched her panties from the pile, kneaded them into a ball and threw them against the wall. Then her bra, her skirt, her T-shirt. The clothes lay strewn around, she fell on her knees, gathered them into her arms, all her mistakes, and sobbed.

In a few minutes she stood up, clear-eyed, and put on the maroon robe they had given. Her tears never lasted long. She always got impatient, even if it was her own melodrama. She walked out without underwear, leaving the clothes sprawled on the floor.

The corridor from the outsiders' bathroom to the door of the Clinic was long and every new entrant had to walk up to the door on their own. She felt like the floor and the wall; they were wearing clothes the same colour.

She pushed the door open. It had a tiny handle and no weight. The introductory video had made such a big deal about 'the last mile' that she expected more of a fight to get in.

On the other side stood Adi, anxious in maroon. Till she walked in he never knew whether she would. Even after all these years he couldn't predict her moods.

They held hands and went to get their underwear. It had all been explained in the video that was mailed to them two weeks ago and they felt like they already knew the place. They took a left and there was the shop manned by couples who were still trying to decide whether to join the programme or not. They worked in pairs, badly synchronised, their hate for each other spilling into their customer service.

One of the men held up a white, plain bra and yelled at his wife, 'Can't you read, it's 34B NOT C'. She snatched the underwear and stormed off into the back of the store. He smiled at the pretty lady he was serving, 'Sorry, she will be back'. None of the couples around judged him. They had all been guilty. Nice to others, monsters at home.

When it was Ira's turn she couldn't remember her exact bra size. The woman who had been yelled at took her to a changing room and asked her to disrobe. With practised ease she measured the rim of her breast, the circumference of her torso, the distance from her nipple to her shoulder. Ira suppressed a giggle. The last time this had happened was at Victoria's Secret.

Ira was a 36B and once she was informed she remembered with perfect clarity that this was her size. Even when her breasts were fine and upstanding they were the same size. The couple who were still making up their mind, gave them two suitcases each, one filled with more uniforms of maroon while the other held correctly sized underwear. Ira couldn't tell if the couple were the kind who would succumb and try the Clinic.

She had heard of cases that stayed ten years and sometimes even more in this no man's land of making-up-their-minds, working without salary, letting their hate fester. She shivered thinking of those people walking out, looking at the world and realising a decade of their life had vanished. For a second, she was tempted to squander what was left on a whim of confusion.

Adi's hand slipped into hers and he asked whether he should carry both her suitcases. She shook her head impatiently and a tornado once again raged in her head, 'Don't smother me. Don't smother me.' She said nothing and walked fast, away from him. He scurried after her; he knew he had done the wrong thing. Again.

It was amazing how they didn't have to ask anybody for anything, that video was fantastic. She walked into a garden, past a small lake where couples were taking turns pushing each other into the cold water. Cries of 'bastard', 'bitch', 'cunt' filled the air. She marched on till she reached her cottage, 7476. Their birth years. They could give their cottage any number in the world and they had chosen this one. It was almost an ATM pin.

There were no locks on the entire campus. If you were having sex and needed privacy you had to put a wooden, green sign outside the door. If you were talking and needed help, you had to pop a red sign out. Ira walked in and wondered what if she mixed up the colours. There were a lot of codes – yellow, purple, orange, brown, lavender. These were the only two she remembered.

This home, her home, their home for an indefinite period of time was a hut, circular in structure, with windows all around. Inside was a double bed, an attached bathroom and a small counter with a toaster, kettle and a single ring hotplate.

Ira dropped her suitcases and ran her hand over the walls. They were made of mud, straw, resins, cow dung. A rough, jutting out pebble scratched her palm and she felt grateful for the fleeting pain. Adi had already thrown himself on the bed and was looking around eagerly. He sometimes reminded her of a large dog, a happy, shaggy, loving beast. Maybe he had forgotten why they were there. Perhaps he felt this was a holiday, a break after two decades of serving in the same company.

She went and lay next to him, oddly touched by his innocence, his acceptance of what they had decided to do. It was a beautiful room, the brown structure, the red oxide floors and the green trees which waved at them continuously from all sides. She suddenly sprung up, bolt straight and checked under the bed. No snakes. That was one of the things they had to look out for, snakes under the bed and scorpions in the bathroom. The mosquitoes had been driven away by the *Kaat Tulasi*. A natural insect repellent, it had been gifted to the Clinic by the tribal people for running a free school for their children. Ira had already decided to steal a few cuttings to take back to the city.

Ira leaned back on the pillow, Adi turned on his side, took a strand of her hair gently, brushed his nose with it and kissed its tips. 'Happy?' he asked with all the love in the world. A groan slid silently down her throat.

Didn't he realise that coming to the Clinic isn't a *happy* occurrence? Even if it was what she had begged for.

Adi fell asleep in their new, circular hut. His breath regular, untroubled. She was the only thing that troubled him. He didn't deserve what she had put him through. She wished he had fallen in love with someone else, someone less temperamental, someone who didn't resent him. She knew she wasn't a cruel person but with him something always happened.

Ira got up to go to the bathroom to wash away unpleasant thoughts with toothpaste or a mouthwash. Over the years Adi had seen her brush her teeth and gargle at the oddest of times and had accepted it without question, as he embraced all that she did. She knew he was still afraid of losing her. She could sometimes see it in his eyes when she walked out of the room and came back.

The bathroom was surprisingly blue. A lime-washed, chalky blue of a sky she hadn't ever seen. She quickly looked around for the black of a scorpion, but there were only the pale yellow geckos running around. She had never been squeamish about reptiles and she didn't flinch when one of them dropped to the ground some distance away.

Two hours later when Adi woke up, the sun had set, the room had changed from a lit-up red to a blackish blood.

'I'm starving. These afternoon naps always double my hunger.'

They walked out towards the canteen. The food was supposed to be good. Vegetarian, organic, simple. On the way they met another couple who looked older than them. The lady had orange hair; loud, defiant and a bit bleached.

Orange hair gave them a full-mouthed grin. Pink gums flashed as she spoke, 'How many years?' Ira blinked, confused. How many years of what? Her problems? Her periods? Adi stepped in, smooth, 'We've been married ten years.'

The orange-haired lady hit her husband's shoulder playfully but it was hard, so hard, he lurched a little as he walked, 'We are 25. This is our Silver Jubilee Anniversary gift to ourselves.' Then she laughed, a sound that held the death rattle of her heart. Adi and Ira walked a little faster, away.

The Clinic was supposed to be their last resort, but Ira doubted that. She had tried so many times to go away but Adi had always reeled her back in. She couldn't understand why the bonds between them wouldn't snap. She had broken up with more men than she could count. From every one of them she had walked away, free. There was no effort, it was like changing clothes. Maybe the difference was that Adi was skin, not fabric.

Her cousin had once listened to her as she listed all of Adi's good points and all of her flaws. This cousin who was single and unpalatably frank had on that day been gentle with Ira, 'You are being too harsh on yourself. Abuse can come in all kinds of forms.' Ira shook her head.

'You can't be abused by goodness, can you?'

Benjamin Stickney Morrison is a second year MFA Prose Fiction student from New Orleans. *LAND* is an upmarket commercial novel that follows Orson Land – the scion of a political dynasty – in his final year at boarding school. *LAND* explores themes of power, family, class, and grief.

LAND
Extract from a novel

CHAPTER 1

I need to find a place to hide Will's letter. It's a nice thick cream envelope, but not too heavy – must only be a page or two. I flip it over; the Brookses' home address is letter pressed into the back of it. He must have gotten it from his mother's stash. I can just imagine his freckled fingers flipping through her desk to find the stationery. I twist it around in my hands – his suicide note – he's written *Mother* in black ink on the front of the envelope in his tight cursive. I lean back against the wall and cross my legs.

My name is Orson Land by the way. Yes, those Lands. Everyone knows of us. It's been this way all eighteen years of my life. It only got worse when I came to St Benedict's – three years ago. Although now I'm a senior, I'll admit I like it.

St Benedict's bell rings, I can hear it from our – well my now – open window, calling all the students to opening chapel in five minutes.

Will's white cotton sheets are folded and waiting on his bed, but he'll never use them again. His family are coming today to get his stuff. I look at the sheets monogrammed with WBE. It'll all be gone by the end of the day.

I get off my bed and lift up my mattress. I rest the letter on the springs towards the back. But as soon as I sit back down, it feels all wrong. No, it'll get crushed if it stays there. I rip the mattress back up – scattering my sheets and comforter – and snatch the letter back.

It's more worn than when I found it, the edges are creased. God knows how many times I've taken it in and out of my blazer pocket, held it in my hands, trying to decide whether to open it. I still haven't decided. I'm surprised my fingerprints haven't imprinted on to it. His family told everyone it was a hunting accident. Let people think it was a hunting accident. I wish it was an accident, I really do, but it doesn't matter now.

Mother stares out at me as I sit down at my desk. I start to put it in the drawer, next to my fresh notebooks and unsharpened *Black Warrior* pencils. No, it can't stay here – anyone could look in my desk – the cleaners or someone trying to borrow my calculator. The letter pulses in my hand. I sit on the floor with my back against the door. Will's trunk sits at the foot of his bed. We always mail our trunks ahead of time, so they're waiting for us in our rooms when we get here. My trunk stands open. The summer before my freshman year, I glued postcards of the Parthenon Frieze – from the British Museum – on the inside lid. I prop the letter up on the bottom lip of my trunk, but my trunk is too obvious a place to hide it. Not that anyone knows it exists.

Our room feels empty without Will. St Benedict's just isn't the same. I miss his stupid laugh, the way his school shirts were always wrinkled, or how his blue eyes sometimes looked purple in the sunlight. We'd been here together for three years, and he decided to leave me to face our senior year alone. I feel like Achilles must have after Hector killed Patroclus. The bell rings out again, signaling three minutes left.

I look to the window – next to it is the St Benedict's School crest framed in gold – shining in the autumn sun. It was my father's when he was here. Navy and green ribbons swirl around the words Fratrum, Nobilitas, et Veritas. Will used to intone the words every morning to wake me up, in Latin. A translation for those not fluent: Brotherhood, Nobility, and Truth.

I pull the frame off the wall. It's already dusty. Nails have been skilfully beaten into the cement between the painted bricks by generations of St Benedict's students. The letter fits perfectly on the inside of the frame, resting against the back of the print. This could work. I take a final look at it, the tight swirls of his writing – he used to hold his left wrist at ninety degrees when he wrote – and set it against the wall. No one would think to look back there. It's almost too good to be true. I feel lighter than I have in days.

Outside, ranks of St Benedict's boys are hurrying towards the chapel, a sea of navy crested blazers, khaki pants, and oxblood penny loafers. Their hands running through their hair or trying to knot their ties before entering the chapel. From the third floor of East House I can see the weaving of the pavement that leads to the quad, manicured lawns that are not for walking on, and trees whose limbs have grown heavy with the weight of summer leaves. East House has the best view out of all the dorms. St Benedict's red brick buildings – some topped with faux Tudor façades – stretch across the landscape, the water tower – black and painted on both sides with the school crest – rises above buildings and trees behind Graves Hall, and the tips of the Blue Ridge Mountains peak out above the wooded hills that surround the campus.

I adjust my tie in the mirror, close the door, and head downstairs. Then I step out into the warm late morning North Carolina sun, and join my classmates processing towards the chapel. I take my time, letting the sun sink into my wool blazer, it's a bit too hot to hurry. And they won't start without me.

—

I swear this school runs like clockwork, they don't miss a beat. As soon as I stepped back on campus, I was whisked away to meet with Dr Bradford – the headmaster – in his office; where after a polite inquisition about how I was after Will's death he said, 'I've talked with your father and we think it's best for St Benedict's if you are named Senior Prefect at tomorrow's assembly. While we are certainly all upset, I think it's for the betterment of the student body if we start the school year off like any other.' His salt-and-pepper moustached mouth moved to form these words, like he was offering me some sort of choice. As if there was another alternative, or that I'd missed his mention of my father's call. Every Land who has attended St Benedict's all the way back to my great-grandfather has been the Senior Prefect – SP for short. Countless great-uncles, cousins, plus my grandfather, father, uncle, and brother all had this distinction. It was a strange twist of fate when Will was chosen as SP for our class, but his string was cut by Atropos, and so my destiny seems to have corrected itself.

So here I am on the dais in Mountford Chapel, as Dr Bradford gives his welcome back address before the actual service begins. My new SP badge shines brightly on my blazer lapel, Bradford gave it to me yesterday, but it's lighter than I imagined it would be. The gold enamel – of the St Benedict's crest encircled with the words Senior Prefect – catches the ceiling lights aimed at the altar, it sends a small golden reflection bouncing across the stained glass and the chapel ceiling when I move. When I was a kid I used to wear my father's old pin, poking holes in all my little polo shirts and pajama tops, it always felt so heavy, as if its weight was pulling me to one side. I should feel like I'm on top of the world.

His missing presence is felt in the whole space, where four-hundred people are crammed into narrow wooden pews. Hyacinth Brooks is seated in the second pew to my right, looking stone-faced and beautiful at the same time. She betrays no emotion. I didn't realize they were coming to chapel, I assumed they'd just collect Will's stuff and go. Zoe – Will's girlfriend – cries quietly next to her. Zoe's chestnut hair isn't in its usual ponytail, it hangs across her face with some strands stuck to her teary cheeks. Hyacinth makes no move to comfort her.

Hyacinth looks distrait, even though her eyes are aimed at Dr Bradford. Her blond hair is cut to match the angle of her jawbone. *Mother* – the letter isn't for me. I reach into my breast pocket. Shit where is the letter! Then I remember it's safe – hidden in my room.

'Now, I'd like to invite this year's Senior Prefect, Orson Land, to say a few words,' Dr Bradford says and steps back.

A lackluster applause follows. I can understand that. All of this is tainted by Will's death.

I don't know whether to smile as I give my speech. I sort of want to, but in the end, I don't. I place my hands firmly on the wooden lectern and let me fingers curl around the smooth edges. A large leather-bound Bible is open to the *Book of Proverbs*. I quickly look to Hyacinth whose face is unchanged in its stoicism.

'It is my great honor to be selected as the Senior Prefect – even under such circumstances. Will was my best friend, ever since we were roommates our freshmen year.'

A funny thing happens when a student dies: everyone is eager to claim them as a close friend. In my case, I really was.

'William Brooks was loved by everyone who met him. He exemplified all of the qualities that make up a St Benedict's man – Fratrum. Nobilitas. Veritas.' I pause to let that sink in. 'Many men in my family have served as Senior Prefects and it is a privilege to be the next in that line. Furthermore, I will strive to carry on Will's commitment to the values of our school.'

Zoe sobs as I finish, and I contemplate walking off the stage to comfort her. But before I can act Sydney Heywood reaches up from behind her offering his handkerchief, and slyly moves to rub her back. So, I just step back and return to my seat behind the altar, all the while watching from the corner of my eye as Sydney's hand moves in small circles – probably feeling for her bra strap.

I imagine Lyndon Johnson must have felt a strange combination of guilt and joy at becoming President. And I can't help but feel this is all destiny falling into place. This outcome was inevitable, my entire childhood my grandfather would sit me on his lap and tell me I would one day go to St Benedict's and become the SP just like him.

Fate, destiny, predestination, call it whatever you like, however you look at it some of us are meant for greatness. Someone must rise to the top. It could be that I've been led here by a golden string, like some sort of Greek hero – Theseus or Odysseus – if history has taught me anything, it's best not to be dragged along, no, I'll walk hand in hand with my destiny.

Victoria Proctor is a comic novelist, whose debut is a dark satire revolving around the life of a wealthy woman in West London. It uses the film *Notting Hill* as a framework. Victoria was born in 1988 and raised around Europe. After graduating from Edinburgh University, with a degree in History of Art and Chinese, she moved to London and became a bartender in high-end hospitality, an experience which has informed her novel.

Notting Hill Two
Extract from a novel

Life was good again, she thought, before driving into a man.

Shit. Screaming, she slammed on the brakes. But it was too late. Lydia felt the front and rear wheels mount him with the ease and skill of an expensive, city-dwelling four-by-four, well-used to inopportune lumps and potholes. They'd barely had time to make eye contact before the bumper struck him squarely, his body crumpling under the force of the collision and folding out of sight below the car.

She breathed out. The street was deserted, but either side were estates packed full of council flats and their inhabitants. Bright lights still shone from the majority of windows: families stayed up later in this neighbourhood. Often, she heard them from her balcony, not a five-minute drive away (although it might as well have been another country), down the desirable end of Portobello Road. Heavy dance music blared, declaring itself the appropriately heart attack-inducing soundtrack to the incident. For a few seconds, she waited. It wouldn't be long before someone arrived. She could hear voices coming from nearby ground-floor flats, doors opening and closing, a woman cursing, dogs barking and in the distance, sirens. They would all come for her.

In her rear-view mirror, she could see the man's contorted form lying in an ever-expanding puddle. A sob escaped her: *fuck*. What was she going to do? For an awful second, she wondered if she might laugh. Giggles bubbled behind her pert, lipsticked lips. She was panicking. Hysterical tremors rippled through her; she held out a hand and watched it buck and fizz. What had he been thinking, walking in the middle of the road like that? She realised she'd been emitting a kind of high-pitched mewling sound. Her wide-shouldered date with the highly-polished signet ring, the glitzy bar, the brass bathroom, the feeling of his lips on hers, all faded into memory. Hitting someone with a car was the worst possible end to her night. She felt terrible.

Three martinis had left her giddy. Now, the alcoholic vapours dispersed. She felt sober and solemn enough to perform any task. Her car had come to rest a little way from its victim. She left the engine running and stepped out into the road. Walking a quick circuit, she could see that the pristine bodywork had been quite ruined by the impact. A dent ran from grille to windscreen and the headlamps had shattered into an incriminating trail on the tarmac. She stooped to collect the larger fragments of multi-coloured glass, unsure as to whether they could be traced back to her or would be taken as a staple in this kind of... 'hood.

The man lay on his back and as she moved to stand over him, a fresh wail escaped her. The kempt silver-brown hair, the delicate nose, thin lips, high cheekbones, just-above-average height and build, all-round perfect-featured, best of Britain charm punched her hard in the stomach.

It was Hugh Grant.

She swore loudly and instantly regretted it.

Grant looked perfectly horrible. He'd broken his neck, judging by the obscene angle of his head. No doubt it'd happened when he'd ricocheted off the bonnet. His face had begun to swell, though not beyond recognition and his nice white shirt was completely transparent and filthy with blood and dirt from the road. Looking up, she caught a fat raindrop in the eye and blinked; what with the accident, she'd barely noticed it was raining. She nudged him reluctantly with the tip of her toe, careful not to get him on her Jimmy Choos. Then, she sighed, she was already soaking wet and irredeemably dirty.

Tears of frustration welled up in her eyes, threatening to bleed out and mix with the rainwater. Killing a normal person was one thing, people could forgive the kind of accident that'd just taken place. Not the family of course, but society. They forgave bad drivers all the time. Hugh Grant had probably had a few DUIs under his belt, back when he was alive. Sure, her licence would be revoked forever, and sure, sometimes a stranger would ask her why she wasn't allowed to drive, after which an awkward silence would descend. Sure, she'd have to perform several hundred hours of community service in an ugly neon tabard and to watch educational videos in an ill-lit classroom, the content of which would probably be shocking photomontages of dead children paraded across the screen, tools in a slow escalation of emotive propaganda. But, all in all, most would chalk the whole thing up to misfortune. She'd been drunk and no doubt he'd been drunk. Why else would he have been in the middle of the road? He'd been asking for it.

Killing Hugh Grant, on the other hand, was tantamount to regicide. She'd spend the rest of her life in prison.

He moaned then, as if in agreement and squinted his eyes open. 'Where am I?'

'Notting Hill,' she whispered in reply. Perhaps it would give him some comfort.

There were only a few things that could happen now: number one, she could drive away, pretending nothing had happened. Grant's half-alive corpse would be left in the road. Later, he would be discovered by a passer-by and they would alert the authorities. During which time, he would hopefully have died.

The police would carry out an investigation, instigating a semi-futile, London-wide search; there had been no witnesses. It was past midnight and in this city of nihilists, nobody gave a fuck. For her own part, she would lie low and mind her own business, focus on the gallery; it wasn't as if she didn't have enough to be getting on with. She had no criminal record, only a few speeding tickets. There was no reason to suspect her. Perhaps she should buy a new car. She couldn't contemplate that: she loved her Range Rover.

The second scenario was the same, only in this one, Grant survived. He would, without flinching, give her up to the police and she would become a national hate figure. Grant would heal at the hands of the most skilled surgeons money could buy, return to film and go on to become even more famous – handsomely scarred. The remainder of her days would be spent behind bars. Grant would show her no mercy.

Number three, she could drive away. Hugh Grant would then drag his battered carcass to the safety of the bushes, where he'd promptly, wonderfully, perish in dignified solitude. His body would be discovered months, if not years, later by some poor gardener trimming the laurel. This was her favourite: the longer Grant's death remained undiscovered, the further she could distance herself from the whole thing. (Perhaps, she could move to Ibiza like she'd always wanted to.) Eventually, it would become impossible to tie a specific vehicle to the bruises. It wasn't as if they could dust for tread marks – or could they? The police would be forced to file the case and chalk it up to a tragic accident. Which it had been, she reasoned, tragic, accidental.

Four, after her driving away, his tattered remains would be discovered by a depraved third party and hidden for reasons as of yet unknown, possibly blackmail. Though an unlikely end to the proceedings, she did have enemies – namely that couple who ran a rival gallery in South Ken, whom she'd been publicly derisive towards.

Finally, he would claw his body to the aforementioned sanctuary of roadside shrubbery, heal in secret, yet be irredeemably disfigured. His only reason to continue living: vengeance. His remaining days would be spent awaiting the opportune moment to annihilate her. He had enough assets to finance several lifetimes of hermitage. She would live out her own life as a fugitive, never sure which mouthful of sashimi was poisoned, which expensive new four-by-four's brake cables had been snipped, which al fresco dining area marked by long-range sniper rifles.

Each option was riddled with uncertainties. Grant moaned again and he seemed to be giving her a look. One thing was undeniable, he'd seen her now. She squatted on her haunches next to him, her own head tilted to the side mimicking his distorted posture. Tenderly, using both hands, she arranged his foppish head in such a way that it looked less unnatural. He moaned again and she ran her fingers through his wet hair.

The rain had slowed to a drizzle. She hopped back into her car to dry off. A woman like her had so much to lose, particularly in the eyes of her Notting Hill set, but also in terms of her basic civil liberties. She'd come so far in the world. By society's standards, she was rich. Her bank account was full, she had everything she needed. But at what cost? Over the years, she'd never allowed herself to become attached, to feel for another human being, for fear that empathy would impinge upon ambition and behind her lay a trail of used bodies like crumpled tissues. Her house would be empty when she arrived home, as it always was. At forty-nine, she was no spring chicken (although most people placed her between thirty-nine to forty-five and she never bothered to correct them). She'd hardened her heart and buried her need for human company deep, until the flame of compassion had become nothing but an oxygen-starved flicker. After tonight though, her date, she recognised something inside of her was changing. She didn't want to call it love, at least not yet.

Smoking furiously, she racked her brain for ideas, remembering with a flash one Christmas, years ago, when she'd watched her sister handle a not dissimilar problem. They'd spent the holiday in a cottage somewhere on the Norfolk Broads. A hideous occasion, marred by excessive drinking on everyone's part and accompanied by the stoic, looping soundtrack of her nephew's tears. One of the days, she and her sister, Tuppence, had gone for a drive, to the shops for more booze no doubt, and struck down a pheasant as it'd shot out from the hedgerow. The stupid animal had still been alive when they'd pulled over to check, eyes gaping, heart beating impossibly fast. Tuppence had been a vision of sangfroid. Explaining gently that it was cruel to leave the beast suffering, her sister had then arranged the flopping bird neatly on the road.

'What can we do about it?' she'd asked.

'It's our duty to put it out of its misery.'

'How? A rock?' She'd made a kind of smashing motion with her fist.

'Don't be vulgar. I'll show you.'

And Tuppence had hopped back into the car and reversed slowly, expertly over the game bird's neck, thereby ending its pain.

That pheasant had been beautiful she remembered, just like Hugh Grant. The green and ruddy feathers bright and shimmering against the sepia-toned landscape, dark tarmac and bleached-out winter sky. Grant wouldn't feel a thing, she told herself as she put the car into reverse, inching back towards him. And as she struggled to load his heavy corpse into the back seat of the Range Rover, she remembered that they'd taken the pheasant home too, to eat later that night.

D.C. Restaino is a writer of short fiction. He is currently working on a collection of stories about the perception of loneliness and its many forms. He also wrote this short bio.

Purpose and Practicality of Congregating:
A Naturalist's Understanding of Combating Loneliness
in the Animal Kingdom
Extract from a short story

On the twenty-third floor of the Oak City Nittochi Nishi-Shinjuku Building in the Shinjuku ward of Tokyo, Japan, Helen is working at her desk.

She pays no attention to the foreign skyline outside. Instead, she focuses on the work before her.

She clears her throat once, then again. She smooths her auburn hair and tightens her ponytail, scrolling back to the top of her advertisement proposal. Briefly, she considers taking a break to listen to the audiobook on animal migration she started on the plane.

At the slide entitled 'Predicted International Impact' she starts reading.

It has been five days since she arrived in this new city, and her body is finally becoming accustomed to the time change from her native Minneapolis.

She picks up a folder from the desk and fans herself. The heat is sticky here. Unlike the time difference, her body won't adapt to the humidity during her short stay in Tokyo.

In the same Nishi-Shinjuku Building as Helen, men head towards the indoor golf driving range for a bit of exercise. Deep beneath the building, the ever-busy Marunouchi Line rumbles on. Ambulance sirens blare as they enter the nearby Tokyo Medical University Hospital. A steady honking of car horns and screeching of breaks permeates the air.

Meanwhile, inside her office on the twenty-third floor, Helen continues to work quietly, swiftly, and alone.

Twice a year, every autumn and spring, across North America and Europe, starlings prepare for their bi-annual migration south. In Denmark, this event is nicknamed Sort Sol, or Black Sun. The sheer number of starlings that cover the sky over the marshlands of Jutland are said nearly to blot out the sun.

A starling murmuration is a true feat of navigational acrobatics. The birds move together, appearing as a gigantic, multi-individual creature. The swarm twists and weaves and folds in on itself, but never once do any of the birds collide. They fly with a precision that makes the Blue Angels envious. They accomplish this by tracking the movements of up to seven of their closest neighbours.

Their flight is maintained by three rules:
- Rule of Separation:
  Steer oneself to avoid crowding or bumping one's neighbours.
- Rule of Alignment:
  Match oneself to the assumed direction of one's neighbours.
- Rule of Maintenance:
  Direct oneself towards the average position of one's neighbours.

The purposes of flocking are many, but, in a migratory sense, the main function is aerodynamic. By arranging themselves in specific shapes, the starlings can take advantage of changing wind patterns, using the surrounding air in the most efficient way.

Using one another, they make their own struggles easier to bear.

Helen rechecks the consumer figures for the ad proposal she input earlier in the day. She is holding a sandwich in one hand.

She plays the rough version of their ad.

A car winds between low, country hills. There is no evident location, but it looks vaguely Scottish. The Highlands, perhaps. The rugged environment suggests wilderness, exploration, a final frontier here on Earth.

Cut to a man in a tailored suit. He smiles, shifting gears.

Cut to a car speeding quickly across the screen, into dense fog, vanishing from view.

The tagline, 'Adventure is Waiting', fades in, before the screen fades to black.

Helen takes a bite of her sandwich. She chews, scrunches her face, and looks at it. There, between the tomato and the ham are thin slices of cucumber.

She hates cucumber. Her father used to tell her that she'd like it when her taste buds matured. She is still waiting.

A knock turns her attention to the door.

'Your smile always manages to brighten my day.' A man leans against the frame of the door, his white teeth set apart from his dark caramel skin. The sleeves of his dress shirt are rolled to his elbows. His hands are in his pockets.

'What do you need?' She puts her sandwich down on the table, sidestepping his effort at humour.

Helen and Mark have worked together off and on for the last eight months. This is their fifth ad campaign together. She enjoys working with him, despite his attempts to make her open up. They divide the work according to their strengths: her organising presentations and calculating figures, him liaising with the creative team and pitching ads to clients.

'Are you coming?'

'We don't have a meeting today.'

'To the breakroom.' He jerks his head left. 'There's gonna be cake.'

'What for?'

'Miko's birthday.' Mark contextualises slowly. 'Miko. The translator. Our translator. She's been working with us since we landed.'

'Of course.'

'So, you'll come?'

'I still have a lot to put together here.'

Mark stands for a moment at the door before making his way to the breakroom by himself.

Every year, millions of wildebeests circle the African plains during the great Serengeti Migration. It occurs without fail, following the same route.

Following the short rains in November, the herds congregate in the south-east quadrant of the Serengeti National Park in Tanzania. Over the next few months, the herds will grow as they graze, give birth, and prepare for their journey. In April, they start to move north.

The migration continues through the summer, traversing plains flourishing with grass and fresh water alongside hordes of zebra and gazelle. Their first river crossing occurs in June when the herd comes across the Grumeti River, more a series of pools and shallow channels when they encounter it.

It is in September, more than halfway through their journey and after migrating into Kenya, that the wildebeests face their greatest threat: the Mara river – its surging, frothy waters still swelling from the late summer rains.

The herds gather at the edge of the waters – waiting, watching for signs of the danger lurking beneath the muddy surface – for the long jaws, the sharp, hooked teeth, that could drag them under without hesitation. All at once, the wildebeests charge into peril.

The survivors feast in celebration on the opposite shore. Then, quickly breaking into smaller herds, they continue their journey. For they still have months before they return to where they started the year before, in the short-grassed plains on the southern tip of the Serengeti. There, they will mate and prepare for their great migration again. For that is all they know. They constantly pursue survival.

The water from the tap is cold. Helen splashes herself twice, rubs her eyes and pushes herself up from the basin. She watches the water drip from her face, swirl around the drain, and rush down the pipe.

She turns to find a towel to dry herself, but only sees hand dryers along the wall. She enters a stall and wipes her face dry using some toilet paper, flushing it when she's done.

Back in her office, she scrolls through her emails. One from her landlord. One from her mother. Most are promotions.

She stops and clicks on an email with no subject line. It's short, informing Helen they left her key in the mailbox. It's simply signed 'Aisha'. Helen remembers not two weeks ago when they signed off with 'Love', and before that 'XOXO'.

She returns to her inbox. She responds to her mother telling her that everything is fine, that she'll be home for Christmas, and that the food is good. She replies to her landlord to let him know that she is fine with the increase in rent if the leaky toilet is fixed before she gets back.

She returns to Aisha's email, reads it again. Then, deletes it.

She packs her bag, turns off her desk lamp and heads for the elevator.

She ignores Mark calling her name, pressing the close door button before anyone else has the chance to enter.

Between May and July off the east coast of South Africa, an unexplained phenomenon known as The Sardine Run takes place.

Ecologically, little is known about this mass migration, as it doesn't happen every year. In fact, in the last fifteen years the run didn't take place in 2003, 2004, 2006, 2013, or 2015. However, when it does occur, it results in a frenzy of excitement that infects every living thing which encounters it.

The main purpose of sardines schooling in such large quantities is protection. They instinctively group together when they feel threatened. This behaviour is a defence mechanism, as lone individuals are more likely to be picked off by predators than while in large groups.

When confronted with an enemy, the sardines put on an underwater ballet that is awe-inspiring, confusing their would-be attackers.

They pirouette, twirl, turn, encircle, disperse, and reconfigure. Anything to get under, above, behind, beside, around, and beyond the danger confronting them. Then, after side-stepping death itself, the school reassembles itself and continues up the coast.

Outside, Helen puts in her earbuds and starts up her audiobook. She lights a cigarette, takes a long drag, holds it in, then breaths out.

She started smoking when she was in university as an excuse to leave parties. Despite the habit, she tells doctors she doesn't smoke.

She extinguishes her cigarette at the entrance of the Nishi-Shinjuku station. She scans her pass and walks to the platform for the Marunochi line. It is crowded with people heading home for the day.

She stands by the door of the car, finding comfort in staying close to an exit. She leans against the cold window until she disembarks at the Shinjuku station.

It is busier here: school children in black gakurans, their collars stiff, scurry past her; a gothic-Lolita pokes her in the head with a frilled umbrella; a station worker yells at the young man rushing past on a skateboard, swerving and weaving between the hordes of people.

Helen turns around, then back again. Finally, she spots a green sign with Yamanote Line printed in English beneath the Japanese. She's caught in a wave of people as they surge into the nearest car. She feels compressed on all sides. She twists, squirms, trying to fold herself back towards the exit, deciding to take the next train. The doors hiss closed, cutting off her escape.

The train jerks, screeches, and picks up speed through the underground. Helen, forced flush against the door, watches as another train glides up next to hers. Inside, people are identically crowded, packed tightly side by side. It twists, turning down a separate tunnel.

The train roars through the earth like thunder. She watches condensation bead on the window until it falls under its own mass. It reminds her of thunderstorms back home. The weight of the clouds pressing down from the sky, lightning creating a cage. Storms always make her feel claustrophobic.

The Globe Skimmer holds the record for the longest migration by any insect. Measuring no more than five centimetres, this species of dragonfly travels nearly eighteen thousand kilometres roundtrip. They can fly nearly seven thousand kilometres without rest and can fly up to sixty-two thousand metres high. Their migration takes them from southern India to Mozambique and Tanzania, with stops in the Maldives and the Seychelles along the way.

The swarm follows the Intertropical Convergence Zone (ITCZ), which aids their flight across the Indian ocean. A narrow stretch of space near the equator, the ITCZ is where the northern and southern trade winds converge, resulting in low atmospheric pressure. The Globe Skimmer uses these trade winds to travel faster and glide longer than normal.

However, it is the resulting storms from the low atmospheric pressure that the dragonflies truly seek. The swarm departs from India to avoid the dry season, as they require fresh water in order to reproduce. They chase storms across the ocean to ensure the birth of the next generation. For it takes at least four generations of Globe Skimmers to complete one migratory cycle. Generations of dragonflies born in one location and dying in another. An existence seemingly doomed never to return home.

At Shibuya station, she flails out of the train, trying to beat the stampede to the surface.

Anita Sharma studied English Language and Literature at the University of Oxford. She currently lives in London.

Quicksilver
Extract from a novel

CHAPTER 1

London, 1809

The driver of the carriage deposited Charles's trunk at the entrance to the house. Charles knocked on the door, the brass head of a lion gaping back at him. It was past midnight. He blinked in the brownish hue of the oil lamps, watching his breath disappear into the light mist. His head and body ached after the long, bone-rattling journey in the mail coach; exhausted, he leaned into the stone pillar beside him to keep his balance. A yellow glow of light slowly appeared in the rooms above as the occupants of the house awakened. Some minutes later, footsteps approached in the hallway, and a slender young man dressed in footman's livery opened the door. He was followed by a man in a sleeping cap and colourful silk dressing gown, whose large form occupied most of the narrow hall. Perhaps it was the light or his tiredness, but the footman, whose clothes, Charles thought, looked too large for him, seemed to smile and look at him briefly with surprise.

'Ah, at last, my dear boy, you must be Charles.' The older man stretched out a plump hand towards Charles and shook his hand vigorously. 'Welcome! Mr Delaunay, pleased to meet you, young man! Your uncle has told me much of your story – a terrible business.'

Delaunay turned to the footman beside him. 'Alessandro, see that Charles's things are taken to his room.'

He rang a large pewter bell, returning it with a flourish to a cabinet in the hallway. Soon afterwards, a maid joined them. The young woman yawned and rubbed the sleep from her eyes.

'Elisabeth, ask cook to prepare something for him to eat.' Delaunay took Charles's hand in his. 'Poor boy, you must be famished after that journey.'

Alessandro began to carry the trunk up the staircase, but it banged so loudly on the wooden stairs, that Delaunay cried out. The case was deposited on the first-floor landing, and Charles was shown into the dining room, where the maid asked him to wait while his supper was prepared.

It was a far grander room than any Charles had ever set foot in. Oil paintings adorned the walls in ornate golden frames: luscious green landscapes, portraits of seated women in silken, diaphanous dresses, and one smaller painting entitled 'Venice – A view of the lagoon'. A solitary silver clock chimed one above the white marble fireplace, with a melodious sound that was then dully echoed by a larger clock in the hallway. Charles caught a glimpse of himself in a gilded mirror above the mantelpiece, his head and upper torso floating in its darkened glass, like a ghost surprised to see its own reflection.

He walked around the room, marvelling at the crystal glassware, admiring the polished ornaments and porcelain figurines. As he reached out a hesitant finger to touch a delicately rendered figure of a young woman, the door opened. Alessandro entered, carrying a large plate covered by a domed silver lid, followed by the maid with a bottle of wine and a jug of fresh milk. They deposited them on the table and silently disappeared from the room.

Charles wondered what had happened to Delaunay and why he had been left alone. An ornate silver candelabra had been lit and the table set for one. He examined the candelabra more closely and saw that there seemed to be two serpents rising from its base, their bodies entwined and their heads meeting in the central column. The flames of the candles wavered, wax dripping onto the delicate silverwork. Charles placed his hands on the gleaming wood of the table. White pools of light shimmered on its surface. The clocks chimed again in the silence; it seemed that the household around him now slept, save for the servants moving noiselessly around him. Charles uncovered the plate to reveal fresh bread and an assortment of cold meats and cheeses. He cut a large slice of the soft bread and piled it high with a yellow cheese and some cold beef and ate quickly, swallowing the food with a large glass of milk. When most of the food had been finished, he sat back in his chair with contentment, and then poured a glass of red wine.

As he drank and gazed around the room, he felt as though the faces in the portraits were observing him. A stern old woman in a black dress in the painting opposite him seemed to whisper that Charles was not one of them, he did not belong among them. Other distinguished faces looked down from the walls and declared that he was not worthy, that he was not of their class. Charles rose from the table, unnerved by his reflection rising up to meet him from every polished surface. He looked at his old black suit and his well-worn boots. The lavishness of the room seemed to make their coarseness even more pronounced. He was merely the son of a village pastor, making his unremarkable arrival in the civilised world.

Alessandro knocked briefly on the door and returned to the room, informing Charles that he would show him to his living quarters. Conscious of the sound of his feet in his heavy boots, Charles followed him and slowly mounted the narrow staircase, by the light of Alessandro's candle. Above them, Charles could see a modest glimmer of light from an open doorway, cascading into the darkness. There were at least three flights of stairs, each landing opening onto parquet floors covered with Turkish carpets. On one floor, he brushed past a Chinese enamelled cabinet, decorated with cherry blossoms and birds of paradise; other floors revealed brightly coloured porcelain vases and miniature landscapes. A door opened and closed in the darkness above them. Charles jumped slightly and looked up, but saw no one.

Finally, they arrived at his room. Alessandro bowed and closed the door softly behind him. His trunk had been set down beside the wall, and there was a table and chair by the window, a wooden armoire and cabinet, a bed and a night-stand. Charles opened a window and breathed in the cold night air. In the darkness, a nightingale's solitary voice rose up to him, while an owl hooted somewhere, flapping its wings suddenly, disturbing the branches in a nearby tree. He shivered and closed the window. The light from the candles flickered and jumped; wax spat into their flames. Shadows loomed and shrank on the walls. He looked around his new surroundings and thought of the room of his childhood, the narrow wooden bed and the tattered plain eiderdown, repaired year after year through the seasons by his sisters, and his modest collection of books. When his mother had died he had inherited all of her books, for during her short life she had always impressed upon him the importance of his education. Following her death, he had spent hours alone with them, his fingers turning the pages that her hands had touched, his eyes reading the words that hers had looked upon. And now, they had mostly been left behind, along with the house where she had raised him.

He took out the small map of the world and the constellations that he had copied from the village's circulating library and unfurled it on the table. And as he had done throughout his childhood, in a low voice he recited the places that he longed to visit, as if he could bring the whole world to him.

In the month since he had received his uncle's letter, he had read it several times, searching for what he could learn of his uncle, to understand the kind of man that he was. He had held its ivory paper in disbelief, the wax seal and the black letters written in the sloping elegant hand seeming as if they were from another world, wondering why, after his uncle's absence for most of his life, he should suddenly have shown any interest in him.

Charles unpacked his newly starched shirts from the trunk. Gently, he unwrapped the copy of Voltaire's poems and the miniature portrait of his mother from the piece of muslin, placing them carefully on the night-stand. He laid out his new dark navy frock coat and matching breeches on the bed, feeling the smooth fabric in his hands, before hanging them in the armoire. Charles had tried them on yesterday with his dress shoes, having borrowed the small mirror from the drawing room at home. Walking around his cramped room, with the looking glass suspended from one arm, he had examined his reflection from several angles, wondering what kind of a figure he would assume in London. With tiredness, he removed his old clothes and boots and put them away in the trunk.

The next morning, he awoke to sunlight flooding his room. He heard the sounds of cries in the street outside, doors opening and closing, footsteps, and voices in the house rising and falling around him. A carriage passed below in the street, rattling the windows. Charles realised from the brightness of the light that it was after eight o'clock and worried that he would be seen as ill-mannered for having slept so late. By this time, usually he would be studying at his desk, or writing lessons for his work as a tutor in the village. He stretched his legs out in the bed, feeling the space around him with his feet, comparing it with the cramped bed of his childhood, which he had outgrown long ago. Someone knocked softly at the door.

'Yes?' Charles rose from the bed and quickly pulled on his breeches, stumbling about his room to put on his shirt.

Alessandro opened the door, lowering his eyes. 'Will you have breakfast, sir? Mr Delaunay has requested your company in the dining room when you are ready?'

'Yes, of course, Alessandro. I will be there shortly.'

'Very good, sir.'

In the sunlight, he could see how slight Alessandro was, a boy of seventeen at the most. His eyes were dark even in this light, Charles observed, and seemed to betray no emotion other than a momentary flicker of sadness, a ripple across the waters of a mountain lake.

Charles waited for Alessandro to leave. He poured water into the basin on the cabinet, undressed and washed with the cloth, wringing the towel, dripping cool water across his body. He dressed into a clean shirt and his new suit. Opposite him, in the mirror, the face of a young gentleman looked back; he was almost handsome. He looked at the portrait of his mother – an innocent girl of eighteen in a blue silk dress, with dark curls falling to her shoulders. It had been painted before she had met his father, she had told him, making a gift of it to him a few months before she died. He remembered the sight of her face in those last days, blue and hollow with illness, the soiled bed sheets wrapped around her. Cholera had come fast to the village, a long summer of it, striking down scores of young children, the elderly and already infirm. Their house had been spared, the doctor had told them, with only their poor mother gone, and not the young child she had just brought into the world.

He lightly kissed the portrait, as if he could summon her into the room, allowing her to enjoy his good fortune, to be present in a household that was more fitting for a woman of her family than that which she had known for the last years of her life. Charles closed the door to his room and descended the stairs, following the sound of voices and laughter.

Kate Vine is a winner of the City Writes competition and her short fiction has been published on DearDamsels.com. She is currently working on *Fireflies*, a novel about three women whose lives converge when each is at a point of crisis. She tweets at @Kate_ElizabethV.

Fireflies

Every night it was something. *Something.* A tingling thought that rose from the depths of her mind, wriggling to the surface and pushing open her eyes. Sofie would look up at the ceiling, immediately alert: she knew what she had to do. Some nights it was quite simple, like closing a door or checking on a child. But this time, there was more to it. Trying not to nudge Jack's restful body, she slid from the bed and grabbed her dressing gown.

Leaving the room to the reassuring sound of her husband's snores, Sofie padded along the landing and down the stairs. They creaked, but she'd figured out where to step so as to cause the least disruption. It was a lesson her sons would do well to learn.

Still on her tiptoes, she made her way to the utility room. From the walls hung dogs' leads and layers of coats; the floor littered with hiking boots and moth-eaten tennis balls. Mud was spattered across the wallpaper, old leaves clinging to the floor and cupboard doors. There was a dampness in the room's every fibre. Sofie no longer noticed.

Her feet pushed deep into her husband's boots – she had a feeling hers were buried beneath an old tricycle somewhere in the corner. It was too dark to rummage. She wondered if she could risk turning on the light outside; she wasn't sure how to get down to the vegetable patch in the dark. The path was throbbing with weeds, the pavement cracking as they burst their way through. She looked back into the house and thought of her children's peaceful faces. No, she mustn't wake everyone up again. Closing the door softly, she headed into the night.

Trying to see with her feet, she felt her way down the path, the chill of the breeze slithering beneath her pyjamas. The outlines of the trees, the grass, the bushes, they shone in black and white. The garden was reduced to edges, humming with activity. Sofie preferred it this way, when it came to life beneath the darkness.

Stepping on what sounded like a snail, Sofie clung to the trunk of a tree, steadying her balance. The crunch of its shell would echo inside her for days. Between the trees wound a spider's web, wet and shining silver, the spider plodding up and down as if disappointed by the evening's events. Its body bulged in a revolting arc; she supposed it must be buoyant with eggs.

Sofie put a hand to her own stomach. It had been more than three years now since she'd last been pregnant, too long. Her husband was right of course, Jack was always right. Their house was as strained as the spider's stomach; drawers didn't close, carpets went unseen for days beneath toys, shoes, cereal bowls. There was no more room, no more money, no more time. But this did nothing to stem her need. Jack might as well have told her not to hunger for food.

It didn't help that she longed for a daughter. She loved her four boys with the force of a thousand battalions and yet the desire pushed on. She was sure that her little girl would take on her very traits, become a small, delicate version of Sofie herself; only innocent, free of the traces life so carelessly imprinted. Stretching her fingers into the night air, Sofie could almost feel her daughter's skin, stroke a finger down her smooth and rosy cheek. But how could she explain this to Jack? She usually adored his practicality, how he moulded even the most chaotic of situations into solid, dependable systems. But he would never understand that for her, this daughter already existed, was already theirs. All they had to do was bring her to life.

Grateful that she couldn't see what had perished beneath her foot, Sofie clawed her way onward. The cold was beginning to cling; she could feel the hairs on her arms standing uncomfortably to attention. The moon watched down over her, judgemental in its glare. But she kept going, she had to.

The vegetable patch was at the back of the garden, just before the chicken coop. Sofie crouched down, surveying the lines of the grid. It felt quite redeeming, to be so alone.

'Sofie!'

His voice cut through her every nerve. She almost leapt out of his boots and stumbled head first into the cabbage square.

'Jesus, Jack!' she hissed, her heart thrumming against her ribcage. 'You nearly gave me a heart attack.'

'I don't bloody care!' he hissed back, his voice much louder than hers. He looked like a drunken scarecrow, his hair pointing in all directions, his dressing gown barely hanging together over his pyjamas. His feet, she noticed, were bare. 'What the hell are you doing out here – it's four o'clock in the morning!'

Sofie sighed, trying to catch her breath. She could already tell that no explanation was going to soothe him.

'It's the carrots,' she said finally, her voice small.

Jack took a long, painful sounding breath.

'Carrots?'

Sofie nodded. She prayed this would be one of those times when Jack pretended to understand, even if he didn't. But her hope was not tangible.

His whole body appeared to be shaking with rage.

'Yes,' she said. 'I couldn't remember if I'd planted them. The local news was on earlier, it said we'd probably had the last frost of the year.'

Jack continued to stare.

'So I thought, well, the carrots are supposed to be planted right after the last frost. I read about it somewhere – I do it every year. But I just couldn't remember if I did them at the weekend.'

There was a further pause. The air around them had taken on an energy of its own, reverberating against her flesh.

'I tried to go to sleep,' she said. 'I did, but it just wasn't working. I had to, you know...' She gave him one last pleading glance. '...check.'

Jack's gaze fell to the ground. Even in the darkness she could see deep, purple crevices forming beneath his eyes. He started to clench and release his fists, his breath pushing into the cold air.

'Sofie,' he said, his voice rigid. 'This has to stop.'

'But I was just— '

'Sofie,' he repeated. 'I know things are strange at the moment. I know you're not working, I know you're restless. But this has – to – stop. Do you understand?'

She hated when he spoke to her like he spoke to the children. That was how he saw her, she knew it, just a child playing up because she was bored. He didn't know what it was like, being a painter who couldn't paint. He went to work each day, typed on his computer and came home again, job done. But her work, her art, it was all that kept her mind alive, kept her distracted from the daughter she could see moving further away as each day passed.

'Sofie?'

'What about the baby?' she said. She couldn't help herself. There could never have been a worse time to say it, and yet it burst from her, autonomous.

Jack positively growled. Part of her wished he would give in to the anger seething inside him, become a real animal amongst the trees and the moonlight, his back arching, his teeth bared. She'd watch as the beast emerged from within; long snout, hardened claws, anger racing through his blood vessels.

Instead he stood before her, severe yet inept. 'I am not discussing that,' he said, quietly. He turned around and began slowly to tread his way back towards the house, his body loose and empty. Sofie knew she should follow him, put a hand on his shoulder and guide him gently back to her.

But she couldn't. She hadn't checked the carrots yet.

—

The next day, Sofie's mind just wasn't with her. Breakfast was a chilly affair; she knew the kids could sense the frustration simmering as their father gulped down his coffee, wincing as it burnt his throat. Sofie tried to act normally, but she could feel his eyes upon her. It was quite a relief when she packed them all out through the front door; Freddie, mild as always, on her hip, the dogs scampering about her ankles.

Sometimes Freddie went to her mother's so she could work, but today, she knew there was no point. Instead she played with him on the floor of the living room, enjoying the simplicity of the brightly coloured building blocks. Freddie had been the easiest of the four by far. He had her round face and golden curls that hung about his cheeks, and he loved to be tickled especially on the soles of his feet. He'd wriggle and writhe, trying desperately to get away, only to sneak back to her, grinning with anticipation. Sofie loved to slide her fingers through his hair, chuck him under the chin. She sometimes caught herself hoping he would cry, so blissful was it to soothe him.

They walked the dogs in the afternoon, Freddie suitably padded in his puffer jacket and lime green wellington boots. He was getting old enough to hold Bernard's lead as they strolled down to the back of the garden. Bernard had to be lifted over the fence himself after Freddie, his old bones no longer willing to brave the climb. He was sometimes a little reluctant to head out into the fields these days, unable as he was to keep up with Emmet. Both younger and smaller, Emmet would bound across the grass after leaves, butterflies, birds too focused on their own chase to see him coming. Next to the tired, brooding Bernard, he seemed the epitome of animal energy, leaping about the fields as if hoping to touch the sky.

Freddie held Sofie's hand as he plodded along. He would start nursery school in the autumn; Sofie could barely face the thought of that little hand in someone else's. She'd thought she'd at least have another one on the way by now, another little hand to hold. She didn't know why Jack was being so stubborn. He'd had the exact same objections before they'd had Freddie, and they'd done just fine.

She set down a blanket across the roots of an old oak tree, and the two of them sat watching out over the acres as Bernard sniffed about them, Emmet trying to nudge his comrade into gear. Sofie wondered if Jack's reluctance was anything to do with her behaviour of late. It was more than her inability to work, it was her inability to settle to anything. She couldn't clean one room of the house without starting on another, she couldn't read a book without picking up two more. Her appetite had lost all rhythm; she found herself bloated at dinner but then starving at midnight. It was how the late night walks had begun – with the desperate craving for chocolate chip cookies.

Only they hadn't had any. She'd had to bake them.

She felt as though life was racing ahead of her, out of her reach, she couldn't stretch far enough to grasp it, wrangle it back within her control. It was all she could do just to keep it in her sights, her heart beating incessantly with the effort. She pulled Freddie in towards her, wrapping his bubbling body into her own. He giggled, grabbed hold of a lock of her hair.

'Mummy, I'm cold,' he said, burrowing into her coat. She put a finger to his cheek, his skin was like ice.

'OK, sweetheart,' she said, propping him back on his feet. 'Let's go.'

Millie Walton is working on her first novel, *The Body Mirror* (working title), which explores the anxieties of a young woman in contemporary London as she struggles to claim a sense of ownership over her own life and identity. The novel is split into two narrative threads that increasingly flow into one another and collide to create an eternal present time.

The Body Mirror
Extract from a novel

When I arrive at The Old Blue Last, the security guard rolls up his sleeves, plunges his hands into my bag and shines a torch in my face. He tells me, once, that I've missed the first act and, twice, to be careful of pickpockets. I assure him I always am. The place is packed with people, all leaning over one another trying to get the disinterested bartenders to look up from their iPhones and serve them a drink. I keep my head down and snake through to the bathroom.

'Can't you see the fucking queue?'

'Just washing my hands,' I say, holding them up as if in evidence of the dirt they've collected. I run the tap until it's steaming hot. The soap dispenser squirts a feeble trickle of foam onto my hands and I rub them furiously together, circling my knuckles and kneading between my fingers. The water burns my skin, but I hold them under until I gasp. The girl next to me frowns. I glance at myself in the mirror, half expecting my eyes to be glowing blue as if by just opening that email, I've triggered some kind of metamorphosis. I pinch the skin of my cheeks and smile: *See, you're fine.*

Lottie grabs me as I'm walking past the bar. 'Rosie, there you are! I tried calling you a bunch of times. Are you all right?'

'I was at work drinks. Why? Do I look weird?'

'No, I just thought you'd be here earlier.'

She's looking at me strangely so I say, 'I did some coke with Ella, then I... got lost.'

She laughs. These are things she understands. 'Nice, well, shall we go outside and have a quick ciggie before they play? It will make you feel better.'

I nod and she takes me by the hand. Her palm's smooth, cold. I want to press it against my cheeks, over my eyes. I want to tell her how much she means to me, but I don't. I follow.

'So funny,' she says when we reach the smoking area, producing a pouch of tobacco from her jacket pocket, 'so many indie kids here. Makes me feel old and uncool. You haven't got any...?' She presses a finger against one nostril and mimes doing a line. I shake my head and register a flicker of disappointment cross her face.

'Fuck it, forgot filters. Oh no, here they are.'

She passes me a white stick to hold while she sprinkles a pinch of tobacco onto a king skin.

'All the shop had,' she laughs hoarsely, 'says something about the neighbourhood, don't ya think?'

She launches seamlessly into a detailed description of her day and I nod along, but the buzz has dissolved and I'm left feeling scooped out, shell-like and distant. There's a rushing sound in my ears, so loud that I can barely hear what she's saying. She continues unaware, pausing occasionally to smile and mouth *Hi!* at someone behind my back.

'Jake's just arrived,' she tells me and continues in the same breath, 'He's useless. Absolutely useless.'

'Who?'

'The intern.'

'Oh right, yeah.'

'And when I asked him what he was doing tonight, just to be polite, obviously I didn't actually care, he rolled his eyes – I know, I know – and was like, wait for it.' Lottie pauses for added drama, sucking hard on the end of her cigarette and blowing the smoke sideways. 'He said: Don't you get bored of asking that question? What the fuck is that supposed to mean?' She applies lip-salve, rubbing her lips together until they're gleaming, her eyes all the time searching for someone else to draw into our conversation. If it was anyone else, I'd feel inadequate.

'No idea,' I say reaching across to pinch the tobacco from her pocket and start rolling another cigarette. She corrects the way I'm holding the paper and then takes over and rolls it for me.

'There are a lot of homeless people around here, aren't there?' I say as casually as I can.

She shrugs. 'These gigs are always in the middle of bloody nowhere.'

'I saw this guy asleep on the pavement on my way here. He was so still. I had to stop and check that he was still breathing.' The lie comes so easily that I almost believe it. 'I wish I'd been able to help him.'

'So sad.' Lottie takes a long drag and puffs a thin stream of smoke above her head. We both watch it dissipate into the air. She drops the end of her cigarette and grounds it beneath her foot. 'So this festival.'

'Escape,' I correct her and she rolls her eyes.

'There's a very small chance I might not be able to come.'

'What? But you have to! I can't go alone.'

'I know and like I said, it's not for definite, but,' she lowers her voice, 'I think I might be put on the next project as assistant producer.'

'That's incredible, Lots. Amazing!' I try really hard, but it still sounds fake.

'Thanks,' she looks at her feet. 'They probably won't accept us anyway.

I reckon it's all incestuous. Have you heard anything?'

'Just the automated email.'

Our eyes meet and for some reason I don't tell her about the picture.

By the time the band play, I'm tired and the rolling monotony of the bass hurts my head. Josh, the singer, Lottie's ex-boyfriend, is grinding against the mic stand so hard that he looks like he might be about to cum. I'd forgotten how crap they are and I wonder whether everyone jumping up and down around me is actually just pretending. I turn hopefully to the guy next to me.

'What?' he shouts. When he looks at me, I realise I know him. We slept together a couple of weeks ago at a mutual friend's birthday party: Charlie or Will. I see something pass over his face and I wonder if he's come to the same realisation.

I grab him by the arm and lean into his ear, 'I said, isn't this great?'

'Oh. Yeah.' He smiles a little cagily and steps back, looking around him as if I might suddenly pounce. *For godssake*, I want to say to him, *you're not that fucking irresistible*. But then I think, perhaps it's not me he's worried about, perhaps it's him. Maybe he likes me. I look at him and think: OK, why not? I could do it again. I lean towards him, but a girl with blonde hair poking out from underneath a beanie pushes her way between us holding two drinks, one of which she hands to Charlie or Will. She looks me up and down, and he kisses her on the cheek. I'm tempted to watch him try to introduce me, but decide that it won't be nearly as much fun as I hope.

'Really great to see you,' I shout at them both and turn back to the bar. I order another gin and tonic and drink it standing in the same place. Josh turns his mic out to the crowd and a few people yell something inaudible back. I try to throw myself into it by closing my eyes and swaying, but it makes me feel worse and, after a while, I stop bothering to move and allow my body to be pushed and pulled by the crowd like a piece of driftwood in the sea. I spot Lottie in the corner. We catch eyes and I mouth, *I'm leaving*. She gives me the thumbs up, blows me a kiss and turns back to the stage, throwing her hips forward and arching her back into the chest of a guy behind her. Another acquaintance who I can't quite remember.

Outside, the night is still and my ears are ringing. An ambulance hurtles past, blinding me with blue. I sit on a step, smoke another cigarette, order an Uber. Across the road, the beam of the street light is flickering. It takes me a few moments to piece together the shadows and flashes of illuminated limbs, to realise that it's a man dancing. One man underneath the street lamp. There isn't any music or none that I can hear, but I can't help feeling that music would only be a distraction, that he's listening and moving to something else. Whirling, stamping. Movements sharp and precise. I stand up and walk to the edge of the pavement so that I can see more clearly, but I don't cross over. The space between us feels somehow significant, somehow crucial to the experience. The light and dark swirl above and around him as he spins. I realise that there's a cigarette in the corner of his mouth and I smile as I let a stream of smoke run from my own lips. Every car, every person that passes is an intrusion. I want to hear his breath, I want him to look up – to see me – to see that I'm watching him.

My cigarette burns between my fingers. I feel a sharp stab of pain as the heat reaches my skin, and I let it fall.

At the same moment, his movements quicken suddenly, becoming almost frenetic. He flings himself wildly. I feel my heart beating with his. He lifts his head and I know then that he's going to catch me. My body's trembling and I wonder if he can feel it too. I imagine his eyes: a deep, dark brown. Familiar somehow. I imagine him smiling slowly, secretively, straight at me. But there's another man walking along the pavement. He crosses in front, obscuring my view and I can't tell whether I've been seen. The man drops his head as he walks, something falls out of his hand and into a hat on the ground that I hadn't noticed before. The dancing man doesn't stop: a raise of the hand in gratitude or by coincidence? Then, oddly, something plucks at the base of my belly. Something like pity or desire. I feel the space between us collapsing, the ground moving as if I'm being dragged, as if he's pulling me closer.

A car horn beeps. My Uber's here. It sounds again and I whirl my head round furiously, deliberately dramatic. I hold up my hand to tell him: *I'm coming.* But I can't leave, not now. *This is ridiculous,* a voice says in my head and suddenly I'm laughing. Yes, why hadn't I considered it before? I take out my phone and press record for less than thirty seconds, watching as the man dances on my screen.

The bus arrives before the sun. The early morning air bites into Rosie's skin and the darkness wavers with the promise of dawn. The woman with the clipboard produces a low beam of light and they follow behind her in a silent line, their feet sinking and sliding in the sand.

A ball of glowing light appears suddenly in the black. As they approach, it grows in size, its arms waving orange and red, puffing smoke into plumes above them, until they're at the foot of it: a monumental tower of flames, devouring what looks like an office block with lines of holes cut to resemble windows. The woman with the clipboard turns to face them, staring round at the half-lit, burning faces.

'Has anyone got any questions?' A few people laugh at this, but the woman waits.

'Will we be told where to go next?'

Anna Wharton has been a print and broadcast journalist for more than 20 years, writing for newspapers including *The Times, The Guardian, The Sunday Times Magazine* and the *Daily Mail*. She has also ghostwritten four memoirs including the Sunday Times Bestseller *Somebody I Used To Know* and Orwell Prize longlisted *CUT*. She is currently working on her debut novel, *The Archivist.*

Rachel

The first kid was definitely an accident, I mean, there was no other way to explain it. That kind of thing just doesn't happen, not like that. The poor kid. The *poor* parents. But anyone who looks after children knows, it only takes a split second for something to go wrong, just that fleeting moment when you turn your head and... well, it doesn't bear thinking about. They found her lying there on the floor of the school hall, her limbs all tangled inside her PE kit, as they would be if you'd fallen from that height. The irony was she was actually a brilliant climber, she belonged to one of those indoor clubs. Her seventh birthday party had even been held at one, and apparently all of the children got a turn to have a climbing lesson with an instructor.

Forensics quickly put up one of those white tents around the body, but the kids had already seen the worst of it. You forget about the blood, too. The school had to get a new floor put down because however much they tried, they just couldn't get the red out of the cracks in the parquet flooring in that particular spot. The school hall was out of action for a week, the PTA fund for the year depleted, and to think they had plans for a new climbing frame for the playground. Still, it wouldn't have felt right after, you know...

Some parents described it as an 'accident waiting to happen.' People always reach for clichés when something so tragic occurs. We all need a way of making sense of the world, whatever age we are. The official verdict from the coroner was 'misadventure', and luckily it happened just before the autumn half-term, which gave everyone a chance to have a week off and put it to the back of their minds.

The second kid, well that was just awful timing, and in front of so many people at the nativity as well. That was the worst bit. No, of course it wasn't. The worst bit was losing another pupil, from Year Two as well, and so close to Christmas.

The tree the school bought was so beautiful – a Norwegian spruce with non-dropping pine needles. Since I heard that I've often wondered whether it might have been better for the poor girl if it'd had fewer needles when it fell on her, though perhaps it wouldn't have made any difference, especially as it wasn't the tree that killed her so much as the bauble – it cut straight through the jugular. At first we thought they'd got everyone out of the way just in time, until someone spotted the patent black shoes poking out from under a bit of tinsel. It took four of the dads to lift the tree off her, and by the time they did, well, it was too late.

The kids had been looking forward to a Christmas lunch in the hall, but that put paid to that. It was all a huge shame. A tragedy. And a bauble, who would imagine something so beautiful, so delicate – so small – could be so lethal? I took all mine off the tree after that, I just couldn't look at them. The little girl had been playing the Angel Gabriel at the time. There had been a bit of a squabble among the girls in Year Two for the starring role; I know Rachel had been disappointed she hadn't got the part.

There were investigations of course because, coming just weeks after the last incident, questions were being asked, quite understandably, especially with it being the same year, all the same children as witnesses. But it was an accident, there's always going to be a risk with trees of that size. Maybe it was Mother Nature getting her own back on us – for the tree, I mean. It's only human to seek explanations in things we can't understand.

Still, they'd had two weeks off for Christmas, and we all thought, new year, new start. Well, you would, wouldn't you? It's the same as 'time's a healer', more clichés to reach out for, but they're there for a reason, because they're true.

I guess after everything that had happened, the school wanted to give the kids something to look forward to, that's why they came up with the idea of a Valentine's Disco. They wouldn't usually have made a fuss about Valentine's Day. They got all the kids involved in decorating the hall, each class had to make these red paper hearts. It was something to take their minds off what had happened because the kids were nervous, quite naturally, you saw the way they hung on a little tighter to Mum or Dad's hand in the playground each morning.

The Valentine's Disco was cancelled on the day, of course it had to be, it couldn't have gone ahead after what happened that afternoon. They found him in the boys' loos, face down on the cold tiles, a pool of blood underneath him, and a couple of green paper towels. That was nothing to do with the scene, but you know what children are like for not putting paper towels into the waste basket. They said he'd been running with scissors, the same scissors they'd been using to cut out those little red paper hearts. That was the ironic thing, because the scissors had gone straight into his – they'd punctured his aorta. Poor William.

By the time all the parents arrived to pick up kids, they were furious, quite rightly.

'There's something wrong with this school!'

'You're picking off our children one by one!'

'There's a serial killer on the loose here!'

Well, that was just ridiculous because everyone knew all visitors had to sign in at reception.

The school was closed for a few days. I suppose with three children killed in the same year, they had more questions to ask than before. The head teacher sent a pamphlet home to all the parents: *When The News is Sad: Talking to Children about Sudden Death*. I explained it all to Rachel as she sat colouring in with felt-tips at the kitchen table. She didn't look up but I know it went in. Many of us parents thought in clichés again – bad luck happens in threes – perhaps it was the only way of carrying on.

There were two more deaths before Easter – twins. I know, awful, and that one really was horrific. But in some ways maybe it was best they went together. Perhaps given everything that had been happening we shouldn't have agreed to that school trip to the pier at Brighton, maybe it was a bad omen, and there are some strong currents in that particular stretch of coastline.

So three plus two makes five and so it was no wonder that Year Two struggled on Sports Day. We were at a disadvantage to start with.

The sun shone that day for us though, which seemed the stroke of luck we sorely needed. I watched Rachel as she hopped inside her sack, giving it all she had. She'd been practising in a pillowcase in our back garden for much of that week. In the end though it was Emily from Oak Class who pipped her to the post for the sack race, and the loudest cheer went up from both her parents, which I thought was a little over the top. I'll admit Rachel had a bit of a meltdown.

'She's fine, she's fine,' I told the other parents, as they stood back with their own kids. 'She's just a bit tired, that's all.'

I knew they understood. These seven year olds, they're all the same really. Well, the ones who are still with us.

Looking back now it's a shame such a sunny day ended how it did. The police had quickly secured the area after little Emily's body was found in the wooden playhouse, inside the same sack she'd beaten Rachel in – a bittersweet moment for her parents. The post-mortem revealed one of those tiny beanbags they'd used for the obstacle race right at the back of her throat. I'll admit, that posed a few questions. Why would she have wanted to try and swallow that? I wouldn't go so far as to say she deserved it but...

The police decided enough was enough though. The BBC did vox pops outside the school, and a splinter group of parents formed and put pressure on the governors to investigate. Didn't they realise that we'd been the victims of nothing more than a string of bad luck?

We were all grateful the end of the school year was only a week away. It had been a tougher year than most.

On the last day of term, I put Rachel to bed.

'Mumma,' she said, 'tell me again the story of how I was made.'

I knelt down beside her bed as she pulled the duvet up under her chin. 'Well,' I began, 'a kind man gave some seeds and a kind lady gave an egg, and the doctors put them together in a tube to make an embryo and put that in my tummy, and then you were mine.'

'And were they really kind?' she asked, looking up at me with that foxy little face that looked nothing like my own.

'The kindest people you could imagine,' I said, smiling.

I kissed her goodnight and pulled the door closed behind me. I didn't let go of the handle until I'd cried all the tears, and it was only then that I crept downstairs. I went into my home office and shut the door behind me, and there I opened the safe I kept locked away in a drawer marked 'private.' I unfolded each yellowing newspaper cutting inside, reading one horrific headline after another, killings going back more than a decade. Then finally, at the bottom of the pile, I came to another sheet of paper, different from the fine newsprint, the logo of the IVF clinic embossed on the top. Just a few details: age, height, eye and hair colour, yet a photograph that matched the news clippings exactly.

I looked up to Rachel's bedroom and felt my heart pull on that invisible string, that direct line to hers.

By the time September came around everything had changed: new town, new start, new uniform.

'I preferred blue,' Rachel said, wriggling inside her new pinafore.

'Green suits you better, darling.'

We walked to school, her tiny hand in mine. I smiled at other parents along the way, we'd need to make friends before it was too late. I'd found the perfect school – an outstanding Ofsted, the pastoral care was so much better. They even had a tennis club. It will be different this time, I told myself.

I busied myself on that first day, I unpacked boxes and found places in the new house for ornaments. I watched the clock, crossing off the minutes towards 3.15pm with pride swelling inside, only we never quite made it. The secretary who called from the school office sounded so shaken.

'Th... there's been an incident,' she said, 'I need to reassure you that Rachel is absolutely fine but... another girl in her class... this... this has never happened before...' She broke down.

It wasn't until I got to the school that I heard the details. Many of the parents questioned how a whole wall of books could come unsecured.

'She might have stood a chance if they'd been reading books,' one mother said to me, 'but they say they were all atlases that fell on her. Talk about the weight of the world, eh?'

I shook my head slowly, as Rachel slipped her little fingers through mine.

'I had a nice first day, Mumma,' she said, smiling up at me as her classmates clung crying to their mothers' knees – I guess they'd known the kid a lot longer than Rachel.

I wanted to give this other mum something to help make sense of it, after all, I'd been there. But there was little I could come up with on the hoof like that.

'An accident waiting to happen,' I said, patting her arm. A cliché yes, but sometimes that's all we've got.

Acknowledgements

Thanks are due to the School of Literature, Drama and Creative Writing at UEA in partnership with Egg Box Publishing for making the UEA MA Creative Writing anthologies possible.

Tiffany Atkinson, Trezza Azzopardi, Stephen Benson, Clare Connors, Andrew Cowan, Alison Donnell, Giles Foden, Sarah Gooderson, Rachel Hore, Kathryn Hughes, Thomas Karshan, Philip Langeskov, Timothy Lawrence-Cave, Jean McNeil, Paul Mills, Jeremy Noel-Tod, Denise Riley, Lisa Robertson, Sophie Robinson, Helen Smith, Rebecca Stott, Henry Sutton, George Szirtes, Matt Taunton, Ian Thomson, Steve Waters, Julia Webb, Naomi Wood.

Nathan Hamilton at UEA Publishing Project, and Emily Benton.

Editorial Committee:
 Justus Flair
 Faye Holder
 Laurence Hardy
 Yin F Lim
 Aaron O'Farrell
 Sureshkumar Pasupula Sekar
 Saloni Prasad
 George Utton

With editorial assistance from:
 Gemma Barry
 Jose Borromeo
 Carmen Morawski
 Robert Smith
 David Restaino

With grateful thanks to all the funders who support the scholarships that support our fiction writers, in particular:
 The UEA Booker Prize Foundation Scholarship
 The Miles Morland Foundation African Scholarship
 The UEA Crowdfunded BAME Writers' Scholarship
 The Kowitz Scholarship
 The Malcolm Bradbury Memorial Scholarship
 The David Higham Scholarship (Prose Fiction)
 The Annabel Abbs Scholarship
 The John Boyne Scholarship
 The Seth Donaldson Memorial Bursary
 The Curtis Brown Award
 The International Bursary

UEA Creative Writing MA Anthology: Prose fiction, 2018

First published by Egg Box Publishing, 2018
Part of UEA Publishing Project Ltd.

A CIP record for this book is available from the British Library.
Printed and bound in the UK by Imprint Digital.

Designed by Emily Benton.
emilybentonbookdesigner.co.uk

Proofread by Sarah Gooderson.
Distributed by NBN International
10 Thornbury Road Plymouth
PL6 7PPT +44 (0)1752 2023102
e.cservs@nbninternational.com

ISBN: 978-1-911343-40-0